Your Good Health

Patsy Collins

Copyright © 2025 Patsy Collins

All rights reserved.
The stories in this book are subject to copyright.
They may not be copied or transmitted in any way
without the permission of the copyright holder,
except for brief quotes used in reviews.

These stories are works of fiction.

ISBN 978-1-914339-54-7

The author can be found at
www.patsycollins.co.uk

Or sign up to her newsletter (and get free stories, as well
as news, offers and competitions).
subscribepage.io/ItLSNa

Contents

1. A Shaggy Dog Story

Aggie had always preferred animals to people. It wasn't that she disliked her family, just that she had nothing in common with them. Her sisters played with dolls in their Wendy house and liked dressing up in frilly dresses.

"We're having a dollies' tea party, do you and Baggsy want to come?" they asked.

"No thanks. We're going to play at being police."

Aggie liked to play outside with her dog and get muddy as she hunted for imaginary clues, or pretended Baggsy was a husky pulling her on a sled.

Mummy liked going shopping and coming home with lots of bags. Aggie was happier traipsing through the local woods, with Baggsy. Daddy spent his spare time watching sports on the telly. Aggie enjoyed trying to teach Baggsy to do tricks. He wasn't very good. His poor eyesight, stumpy legs and huge feet made him clumsy but, as Mummy said, those things weren't his fault and didn't make him any less loveable. Aggie didn't mind, she loved her frizzy haired pet.

The children at school teased Aggie. It wasn't just because she was short with frizzy hair and big thick glasses and enormous feet. It wasn't even because she had red blotchy skin due to eczema. They said she smelt 'funny' and laughed at the pet hairs on her clothes. Mummy told her to ignore them, so that's what Aggie did. She made no close friends, but didn't really mind; she quietly got on with her lessons, and then raced home to Baggsy. She did mind when, in her teens, Baggsy died. When she arrived at school with red eyes, she hadn't, as she'd feared, been laughed at. Most children said nothing, but a few, those who had dogs themselves, were quite kind to her.

When she left school, she knew she wanted to work with dogs. Her classmates and sisters worked in shops or started hairdressing apprenticeships. Aggie's own job wasn't so different. She worked in a pet shop, one that provided a grooming service. Aggie hadn't owned another dog since Baggsy, but when she was offered a free Afghan puppy, she couldn't refuse.

"She's no good for showing, because she's got a wonky ear, but she'll still make a lovely pet and I know you'll take good care of her, Aggie," the puppy's breeder said.

"Oh, she's beautiful," Aggie said. She was smitten immediately.

Aggie named her adorable new pet Suki. As she combed the dog's silky blonde hair she couldn't help comparing her to Baggsy. It was often said that people grew to look like their pets. Aggie had seen examples of that herself with her customers. She vaguely wondered if she'd suddenly develop long slender legs or get the urge to bleach her hair. Suki gradually changed from a cute puppy into a beautiful dog. Aggie stayed exactly the same. Well, almost exactly – it seemed her childhood eczema was back. Red patches developed on her arms. Aggie was mildly annoyed, because she'd thought she'd grown out of the condition, but not too bothered by the small red circles. She covered them whilst grooming dogs at work, so the dog shampoo didn't irritate her skin. She used moisturising cream, as that had always helped when she was younger. The patches grew bigger, spreading out in a perfect circle, like fairy rings on the lawn.

One day, whilst grooming Suki, Aggie noticed a small red circle on her pet's skin. Over the next few days, the patch grew a little larger. There were flakes of skin as though the dog had dandruff. Her hair broke off from the affected circle leaving a bald patch. Aggie guessed that her own rash wasn't eczema at all, but something contagious. The following day Suki began to scratch at the mark and Aggie spotted a second one. She rang the vet and made an appointment for that afternoon.

"What seems to be the trouble?" the vet asked.

"I think Suki has caught some kind of rash from me," Aggie explained. She showed the vet Suki's original spot. It was, by then, looking inflamed around the edge with a paler centre.

"Ringworm," the vet declared.

"Oh. I've heard of that but never actually seen it, before. It's not actually a worm, is it?"

"No, it's a fungal infection."

"Like fairy rings on a lawn?"

"Yes, sort of."

"Can you treat Suki?"

"No problem. I'll prescribe some cream. Just apply it on any patches of ringworm and the surrounding skin. It will still be contagious for a couple of weeks, so try to keep her away from other dogs and don't let people handle her unless they're wearing gloves. Keep using the cream twice a day and continue for at least a week after the skin is clear. You might want to use a halo collar if she tries licking the affected area. We can lend you one if you like."

"OK, thanks."

"You said she got it from you?"

Aggie nodded and rolled up her sleeve.

"You'll need to get treatment for yourself too, Aggie."

"I suppose so, or I'll give her the infection again. Oh no!"

"What's wrong?"

"I've been grooming dogs at work. I wore long rubber gloves, but could they still have caught it?"

"The gloves should have protected them, but it is very contagious."

"I'll contact all my customers and warn them to check. Can I use the same cream as Suki, or will I need to see my doctor?"

"You'll need your own cream. In theory the same one might work, but I can't recommend it. You needn't see the doctor though. Just go along to the pharmacist and they'll suggest something suitable."

Aggie went to the chemist as soon as she'd taken Suki home.

"How can I help?" the pharmacist asked.

"I've got this rash," Aggie said and began rolling up her sleeve.

"Would you like to step over here?" the pharmacist suggested and guided Aggie to a quiet corner behind a screen.

Aggie revealed her arm. "My dog's got it too. The vet said it's ringworm and given me some cream for her. He said you'd have some for me?"

"The vet is right on both counts," he assured her. "You do have ringworm and we can supply an anti-fungal cream to treat it." He found the treatment and explained how to use it.

Aggie smiled. "That's easy to remember, it's just the same treatment as for Suki."

"That's convenient. You should try not to scratch the rash. I'm not sure how you'll persuade the dog not to do that."

"I've got a special collar for her."

"Oh, one of those lampshade things?"

Aggie saw he was trying to suppress a smile as he asked.

"Yes, it's very undignified. She's not going to like that."

The pharmacist laughed. "Poor dog. At least you won't have to put up with that sort of inconvenience yourself. You just need to take precautions not to pass on the infection. The ringworm will still be contagious for a while. You shouldn't share towels or allow others to touch the ringworm."

"That's no problem, as it's just me and Suki. Thanks for your help."

"No trouble at all. I was wondering if I'd be able to see your dog. It would be interesting to compare how you both respond to the treatment."

"I often walk her down this way. I'll call in next time I come by."

Aggie rang work and arranged to take her holiday early to avoid the risk of spreading the infection. She felt perfectly well, so enjoyed taking lots of long walks with Suki. Quite often the walks took her past the chemist shop and the friendly pharmacist always came out for a chat.

As her rash subsided Aggie confessed she was almost sad.

He started to say something at the same time as she continued, "You know what they say about owners and dogs looking alike? We did in a way for a little while – oh well, I'll never be as beautiful as her but I suppose we'll both look better once this is properly cleared up."

"Yes, I suppose …"

"Sorry, you started to say something."

"Oh, yes. Me too – when you said you'd be a bit sad once the ringworm had totally cleared."

"You don't want us to recover?" That seemed unlikely given his job, the fact he'd been so helpful to her, and took such an interest in Suki.

"No. I hate the idea that you'll stop coming by to show me."

"Oh."

"Yes, it will be better for you both when it's gone. And yes, I suppose you'll have even less in common when it comes to looks, but you'll both be beautiful in different ways. Suki's blonde fur and brown eyes are pretty, but no more so than your blue ones and lovely dark curls."

"Oh!"

Aggie and Suki eventually made a complete recovery from the ringworm and there are now no traces left. Suki's hair has grown back over the patches and is just as silky as ever. Aggie's own hair is also becoming slightly more silky. She's started conditioning it now that she and Suki share their weekend walks with Fraser, the pharmacist.

2. Spotting The Problem

Simon loved his job in IT support, because he loved computers. He loved downloading the latest music, loved chatting to his internet buddies around the world on equal terms without having to show his ugly, spotty, face. Computers weren't just for the fun stuff though, they were a serious tool and he used them as such. He appreciated being able to look things up and get immediate answers. You could even use a computer to find out how to fix a computer! He valued the way they always did whatever was asked of them, no complaining and no offered opinions. Simon modelled himself on his beloved machines. He was ambitious, and intended to become head of IT and replace his current boss when Harold retired.

Simon was pleased that whenever there was a computer query he was always the person people asked for. He'd built up a reputation for himself, not just in problem solving, but also for his friendly, approachable manner and good advice.

It could be anything from a sticky key to a complete crash. "Get the boy to have a look at it," was the usual advice whenever anyone had a problem.

"Thanks, lad," he'd be told by the marketing manager after he'd retrieved some data the man had accidentally deleted. "Saved hours of work for the team that has. I really appreciate you working through lunch. You're boss ought to let you go home early for that. I'll have a word."

The marketing man might just as well have offered to have Simon let out early to play. Most of the company's staff obviously considered him to be a child. At least Harold didn't see him that way. He knew how hard Simon worked, how much attention he'd paid to Harold's advice. Simon knew about computers from college, but he didn't know much about people. Harold had taught him how to deal with them.

"You've got to know how to handle them, lad. You can't treat them as though they're stupid, but you can't assume they've actually checked the thing is plugged in either."

He showed Simon how to question his clients in order to diagnose the problem. He taught him how to help them get the most from their computers and how to offer advice. In short, he was teaching Simon how to become his replacement. If Harold had been told about Simon working through lunch he'd have been pleased with his dedication and known the reason for it. It was just a shame that the others didn't see him in the same way.

The other staff often made comments about youngsters being brought up to understand technology and how if they couldn't programme a piece of tech they'd get the six-year-old next door to do it. Every time Simon answered his phone, they'd be knowing looks, 'kids these days can't cope without their mobiles' was the thought in their minds. They didn't notice that whilst most of the middle aged women in the office used their phones to gossip, Simon's calls were all work related. They didn't appreciate his skill. Instead they considered it the natural ability of youth. They were quick to praise Harold though. Simon knew what the problem was. He looked like a schoolboy still, because of his acne. Schoolkids had acne, geeky spotty boys who were good with computers. Clear skinned, bald headed Harold was an IT expert with the job and prestige to match. Pimply Simon was a bright kid who loved messing about with chips and wires.

The other staff didn't dislike him. They weren't unkind. They simply didn't recognise him as an adult. Unfortunately his acne wasn't as simple to fix as a loose connection to a motherboard, or a line of corrupted code. To be fair many people did try to help him.

"You don't want to spend all your time cooped up indoors, young man," the lady who served his lunch in the canteen said. "Get out in the sunshine, it'll do you and your complexion good. I could make you up a nice picnic, with brown bread sandwiches and fruit."

"Thanks, but this is fine," Simon had replied, as he picked up his tray laden with fish and chips, a can of Coke and a chocolate cake for dessert.

As he ate, Simon wondered if she had a point. His computer would provide the answer. Once he'd eaten he returned, early, to his office and typed a few keywords into Google. He soon learnt that exposure to sunshine as a cure for spots was a myth, with no evidence to support it. The same was true of his diet. Less chocolate and more fruit would be a good idea, but they weren't likely to clear his skin. Whilst he read this information he remembered the teasing he'd got as a kid. Some people reckoned his skin was inflamed because it was dirty. In common with many boys he'd not been fond of soap and water, but these days he washed regularly and thoroughly, scrubbing at his blackheads, hoping to wash them away. It hadn't worked. Simon checked up on the relationship between hygiene and acne and learnt that he'd probably made things worse rather than better with his rigorous cleaning sessions. His mum had told him that nothing could be done about his spots, he'd just have to put up with it for a year or so until he grew out of it. Apparently, she'd been at least partly wrong too.

"Simon, when you're finished whatever you're working on, there's some literature here I'd like you to take a look at," Harold said.

Simon glanced guiltily at the clock, he hadn't realised that the lunch break was over and his boss was back in the office.

"Sorry, Harold. I hadn't noticed the time."

"There's no rush, it'll keep 'til you're ready."

"I'm ready now," Simon said deciding that honesty was best. "I wasn't actually working, just looking something up for myself and I …"

"Must be something interesting then, let's see." Harold looked over Simon's shoulder. "Acne? Crikey son, I though you'd be chatting up girls or something to get you distracted from work."

"Girls don't seem to like pus and blackheads."

"No, maybe not. So, have you found out how to cure it?"

"No, only how not too. The only good news I've found is that it's not catching and I don't have to worry about worrying about it."

"You've lost me, Simon."

"Stress doesn't make it worse."

"Ah, I see. Wouldn't you be better off finding out what does, or a cure?" Harold asked.

Simon closed down the page he had been reading. "Good idea, but how?"

"Come on, what have I taught you about computers? You've got to approach things the right way. What site were you looking at?"

"One on urban myths."

"Well, myths are no good are they? Would you try some old wives tale to fix a flickering monitor?"

"No, of course not, I'd check in the manual, or get onto the manufacturers. They're the experts who know …"

"So, who'd be the experts in the case of a medical problem?"

"A doctor? It doesn't seem worth bothering. I'm not ill, or even in pain, it's just a bit sore sometimes. Anyway, I did read that what my mum said about growing out of it was right. It will get better on its own eventually."

"Most kids do seem to grow out of it quickly, but that didn't happen to you. It obviously bothers you, or you'd not let it distract you from work. Do you want to put up with it for years?"

"No." Simon sighed. "I'll ring the doctor shall I?"

"Perhaps, but let's not give up on our good friend the internet just yet." Harold leant over Simon and typed 'National Health Service' into the browser. "I used this site myself a while ago."

"Oh. What was wrong?"

"Something I don't want to talk about and I definitely didn't want some doctor looking at if I didn't need to. Anyway, never you mind about me. Thing is this site has advice on every medical condition you can think of, and loads you've never heard of. Think you can cope now?"

Simon very quickly found pages of information about acne. He was pleased to find that there were several different cures to choose from – some of which he'd already tried, some he'd not heard of. He decided he'd get some benzoyl peroxide cream from the chemist. That sounded like it'd be the most effective method without needing a prescription. If it didn't work, he still had the option of going to the doctor for something stronger.

"How are you getting on?" Harold soon asked.

"Good, I think I've found something that will work. I'll buy it on the way home. Thanks for helping, Harold."

"I'm just glad you've got the answer and we can get on with some work. I take it we can?"

They were interrupted by the phone. Harold answered.

"You'd better get down to accounts. Miss Jenkins has got what sounds like the blue screen of death. The NHS can't help you there, lad. This one is all down to you."

3. Don't Get Lippy

His wife Lisa asked a question, as he let himself into the house.

"Yes please, love," Geoff said. He noticed her puzzled expression. "Sorry, I was thinking about my writing group. The speaker was really interesting."

"Oh, you listened to him, then?"

"Of course. Writers have to listen all the time; that's one of the things the speaker was saying. Ideas can be anywhere. I don't know where you get the idea I don't listen."

Lisa shrugged. "Would you like some tea?"

"Yes please, love," he said very slowly and carefully, to make sure she understood him this time. Again he noticed her expression. "I'll make it shall I?"

He handed Lisa the leaflet he'd been given about finding good subjects to write about and wandered into the kitchen.

Lisa read it. He'd been right, it did say that writers should listen. It also said that ideas which sounded exciting might not be and that sometimes it would be better to choose a less obvious subject. The sheet quoted as an example the horrendous sounding medical condition, pityriasis rosea and a small plastic clip – which would the group choose to write about? The leaflet pointed out that the medical condition was really a harmless rash, the plastic clip played a vital role in keeping aircraft in the sky. At first glance, the clip might not have sounded promising, but it might well provide inspiration for a dramatic story.

"I can't wait to get started on my next project," Geoff called.

"What is it?"

"We were given a list of words to pick from and write a story about. Most of us didn't know what any of them meant, but he said that didn't matter, we could research them."

"What word did you choose?"

"That's where I was clever," Geoff said like an author nominated for the Booker prize. "The list was divided into medical conditions, plant names and different types of plastic clips. Which do you think I chose?"

"Was one of the plants something poisonous?"

"No. I didn't think of that."

"A new cure for cancer?"

"No," Geoff sounded slightly annoyed. "I selected a medical condition. The speaker mentioned that earlier, and straight away I thought of someone with a life-threatening condition who has a large family to provide for. He'd be rushing for treatment and there'll be a disaster and he nearly won't make it. Then there'll be an extremely tense surgical scene and then a touchingly emotional one as his family wait for the news."

"That does sound good. What's the condition? Maybe I can help with the research?"

"Thanks, love. I knew you'd want to help, that's why I chose the condition I did. I remember you talking about it.

There's no point in having a pathologist for a wife if I don't use her experience in my writing, is there?"

"I'd have thought there were plenty of advantages to having me as a wife, whatever my profession and your hobby." Lisa said that at a volume even Geoff couldn't avoid listening to.

"Yes. Sorry. Anyway, the point I was trying to make is that you'd told me about this condition and I listened."

Lisa smiled. "Sorry, love. I didn't mean to snap. It's just that sometimes I feel you don't take any notice of me and the real world because you're too busy concentrating on your stories."

They hugged and sat quietly for a while drinking their tea.

"So, what's this medical condition, then?" Lisa asked.

"Lipoma. Do you remember telling me about it?"

"Yes, I do. Do you?"

Geoff heard the warning in her voice.

"Of course. Well, not all the details. Perhaps I could ask you a few questions?"

"Yes. Why don't you write down the answers so I know you're paying attention?"

"OK." Geoff fetched a pen and notebook, feeling rather guilty. He remembered Lisa saying the word lipoma. He'd been attempting to write poetry at the time and guessed his mind had wandered away from what she was saying and he'd been trying to find rhymes. Oklahoma would work. Oh dear, he was doing it again.

"How many sufferers die from it?" he asked.

"I shouldn't imagine many of them would."

"It wasn't one of the bodies you were examining that had this?"

"No, Geoff. It wasn't. It was me. Still is."

Geoff felt sick. Lisa had mentioned she'd found some kind of small lump a couple of months ago. He'd thought she'd said it was nothing. How could he not have listened about something so important? He took a deep breath. She said most people didn't die of it; there was a chance she'd be OK.

"What's the cure?" he asked.

"Usually there's none."

"But, I …"

"You weren't listening when I told you about it, were you?"

Geoff shook his head. "I'm really sorry, love. It's not that I don't care. Please tell me about it now. I feel terrible that there's something wrong with you and I didn't take any interest."

"It's nothing really."

Geoff relaxed a little; he'd thought that's what she'd said.

"Are you sure?"

"Yes. And I'm sure you'll want all the details for your writing… I knew what it was because of my job, of course, but most people would want to see their GP to get a diagnosis. It's just a small fatty lump. Mine's on my shoulder, just under the skin, but they can occur anywhere, even internally."

"And nothing can be done about them?"

"They can be removed, but usually there's no need and it's best to just leave them. Sometimes they might cause some pain if they're on a nerve, or they might be distressing if they're visible. I don't think mine is particularly unsightly."

"No, not at all," said Geoff, who'd not even noticed it.

"But mine's only small and not in a noticeable position. I have examined people who had several or had them on their face or arms. I might feel differently if mine was easily seen. In cases like that, they can be removed."

"An operation?"

"A small one. It's done under local anaesthetic. The skin is lifted, the lipoma cut out and the skin stitched. There would only be a tiny scar. Usually there's no need though."

"What about internal ones, would they be more serious?"

"I don't think most people would even know if they'd got one. They can sometimes cause trouble and so would be removed. If one was found then it might be removed to check it wasn't cancerous."

"So they can become cancerous?" Geoff's concern for his wife cancelled out his excitement over a possible story line.

"It's not at all likely. Some experts think it might be possible, but there isn't any evidence it has ever happened. If there's any doubt over the diagnosis, the doctor would check the lump to be sure it was really just a lipoma and not anything more serious."

"And there's no doubt about yours?"

"No, none."

"Will it go away or change?"

"No, I don't think so."

"So these lipomas; don't hurt, don't make you ill, don't need treatment?"

"That's about it. Sorry, that's not much good is it?"

"Of course it is! It's excellent news. I wouldn't want you to be in pain or needing unpleasant treatments."

"Thanks, Geoff, but I meant for your story."

"Oh. I see what you mean. No, I don't think anyone could make a story out of… Unless… Are they rare? Maybe I could make something out of that."

"They're quite common I'm afraid. About one in a hundred people have one or two. They can occur at any age to anyone. That's not helping is it?"

"No, it's no good at all. Can you imagine it? 'Once upon a time our gallant hero got a lipoma, it was nothing to worry about, so after popping in to see the doctor to get it checked, he carried on just as usual. The End'. That's not very exciting is it?"

"Not yet, but what difference did the visit to the doctors make? Maybe he saw something on his way back to work that he wouldn't have otherwise witnessed?"

Geoff and Lisa discussed possibilities. Geoff listened carefully to every suggestion and eventually wrote an exhilarating story about a man whose visit to the doctors meant he saw a gang go into the bank and take the entire staff prisoner. The gallant hero rescued them all and foiled the evil gang.

"So, how did it go, Geoff?" Lisa asked her husband, as he let himself into the house after the next writing group meeting.

"Brilliant. They couldn't believe that I'd managed to get a story out of such an uninteresting subject. I told them how it was all due to listening to my wife. Not that your great story ideas and help with research are your only good points off course."

"Did I hear that right?"

"Shouldn't think so, you never listen to a word I say." Geoff winked as he said that and quickly offered to make the tea.

4. The Odd Sock

Janet found a pink, floral patterned sock on the stairs.

"Whose is this?" she asked the empty house.

It definitely wasn't hers or Rory's. The only other possibility was their daughter Michaela. She used to wear pretty clothes, but stopped recently. These last few weeks Mickie, as she now preferred to be called although Janet had no idea why, had kept her femininity well hidden. So how did a girly sock end up on the stairs?

The cat could have stolen it from a neighbour and brought it back as a trophy. A freak gust of wind could have blown it in. Rory might have started cross dressing. An alien landing? Except they didn't have a cat, there wasn't a window in the stairwell, Rory's feet were size ten and aliens probably had suckers instead of toes.

Not that Rory was likely to have started wearing women's clothes, or be hiding anything from her. They were very close and talked about everything. The same used to be true of Mickie. All of it.

Mickie no longer dressed as a typical young woman and didn't confide in her mother. Mickie wasn't a cross dresser either – more a sack of potatoes dresser. All her newest clothes were shapeless and covered her completely. Clearly something was going on there, but Janet tried not to let her imagination run away with her. If she did, she'd convince herself Mickie had a horrible medical condition she was attempting to hide even from herself, or that she was self harming, or injecting herself with drugs…

One day Michaela had come home from school, raced upstairs, banged and stomped about in her room for some time, then come down having changed out of her uniform. Instead of her usual ripped jeans, strappy sandals and lacy top, she wore a baggy tracksuit. Janet had bought it for her when she'd taken up jogging, but it hadn't got much use. As Michaela had later confided, the whole point of jogging was so she could be seen in her short shorts and clingy top going past a certain person's home. The infatuation, and therefore the interest in exercise, had quickly fizzled out.

"Everything OK, love?" Janet asked when Mickie appeared in the tracksuit.

"Fine."

It wasn't. Mickie didn't share a single detail about her day and hardly touched her tea. "Whatever's wrong, you can talk to me. You do know that?"

"You think there's something wrong with me?"

"I didn't mean it like that, love. You just seem upset."

Mickie hadn't responded.

"Growing up can be hard. People go through so many changes, sometimes really big ones. And you feel under pressure to conform. You don't have to. Be the person you want to be, whether that's Michaela or Mickie, and don't let people push you into being something you're not."

"Even if they're right?"

Janet desperately wanted to coax out of her who might be right about what, but didn't want to push her into talking before she was ready. Since then Mickie continued to cover herself up, despite often looking very hot and uncomfortable, but otherwise seemed OK. Hopefully it was just a strange teenage phase.

Could the sock belong to one of Mickie's friends? That was possible, but none had visited lately as far as she knew. And even if they'd come round and removed it for some reason, wouldn't they have put it back on again before leaving? Was Mickie a kleptomaniac? Had she started taking in washing? They did seem to be going through detergent quite fast…

Janet was still pondering the mystery of the sock when her sister rang. Janet explained what she'd found and asked Liza if she had any ideas as to how it ended up on the stairs.

"Rory's bought you some clothes as a present? He might have …"

"It had been worn," Janet interrupted. "Ugh. Why did I torture myself with this?"

"You can't think he's cheating on you!"

"No. I meant I sniffed it and it was sweaty. Hey, you don't think that do you? That Rory could be cheating …?"

"No, the man adores you. But on the face of it, that is a likely explanation. This was clearly worn, presumably by a woman, and removed in your house. A lot of wives might have jumped to that conclusion."

"I've been jumping to a lot of conclusions," Janet confessed. "I'm going to keep doing it unless I ask, aren't I?"

"You're not seriously going to ask Rory if he's having an affair?"

"No, silly. I'll ask Mickie what's wrong. I'm intrigued about the sock and want to know how it got there, but that's not the real problem. I'm worried sick about my darling daughter."

Janet put the sock out of sight, resisted looking in Mickie's room, and tried to think of other things.

When her daughter came home, Janet asked her to sit down. "There's something I need to ask you. I should have done it before, but initially I was hurt. Now I feel me not knowing, perhaps not seeming interested, has put a distance between us."

"I've hurt you?"

"Not on purpose and I don't mind now, but I chose your name and can't help thinking of you as Michaela, so it felt as though you were rejecting me when you changed it to Mickie."

"Oh, Mum! It was silly of me to do it. Some girls at school teased me a bit, comparing me to Michaela Strachan. She's small and slim and pretty. I'm nothing like her, am I?"

"Not in looks, no. You have that same inquisitive nature and bubbly personality."

"You mean I used to. I let what people think get to me too much. You remember what you said about not letting people push me into being something I'm not?"

"I do."

"Sometimes that's right, but sometimes they are. At first my reaction to being compared to Michaela Strachan was to call myself Mickie and be as unlike her as possible, not let them push me into changing. Then I realised I wasn't happy. I did want to be more like her. Not short and blonde and on TV, but in some ways. Sorry."

"Why are you sorry?"

"Because you don't want me to change and I'm trying to."

"Oh, love it's not that I don't want you to change. I do because you're not happy and more than anything else, that's what I want for you. Come on, tell me how I can help."

"Less sausages and chips and more salad for tea?"

"I don't follow you."

"I'm trying to lose weight and get fit. I'm doing some exercise, but it makes so much noise in the house and when I go out I don't want people seeing me wobble so I cover up – and then get too hot to do much."

"That explains the tracksuit, but not all your other clothes."

"My usual stuff was getting tight and after what you said, I tried to hide what I was doing. I got it into my head you'd think I'd become obsessed with a celebrity, or was anorexic or something and try to stop me. Now I realise that was as daft as changing my name and I should just have explained properly. With your help I know I'll lose much more than I have already."

"Which is?"

"One sock! I've been washing the stuff I use to exercise in, so you didn't know. Somehow I lost a pink flowery sock." Michaela grinned. "Good thing you didn't find it. With your imagination you'd have jumped to all kinds of weird conclusions about how it got there."

5. Recipe For Happiness

Aiofe Bosham dragged herself out of bed and went through the motions of washing, dressing and eating breakfast. Somehow she made herself leave the house. She tapped her date of birth into the machine at the doctor's surgery and took a seat in the waiting room. After a while the robotic voice called her name, mispronouncing it as usual.

The doctor was a youngish woman Aiofe had never seen before. She looked up and smiled as Aiofe stepped into the consulting room. "Aiofe Bosham?"

Aiofe nodded, both to indicate that's who she was and that Ee-fa Bos-am was the correct way to say it.

"Please take a seat." The doctor smiled again. Not a big grin. Just a slight, reassuring, curve to her lips.

As Aiofe sat she felt… something.

"Why are you here today, Aiofe?"

"The chemist said you wouldn't renew my prescription unless I came in."

"I see. And you want more of the anti-depressants?"

Aiofe nodded. She wouldn't have left the house if she didn't need them.

"Are they working for you?"

"I suppose." They allowed her to trudge through the day. Since taking them she'd kept herself and the house clean, fed herself – things she'd previously given up on.

"And are you happy?"

Aiofe had no answer.

"I'll renew your prescription, but you need something else."

That sensation Aiofe had first experienced when she'd first seen the new doctor reappeared – or perhaps hadn't gone. Was it hope she felt as the sheet of paper was handed to her?

Aoife had to read the list – flour, butter, sugar, eggs and jam, twice to be sure her eyes weren't playing tricks. The words below made no more sense. "I don't understand. This is a recipe… for cake. Isn't that bad for us?"

"Not in moderation. Please, will you trust me and just try it?"

Aiofe, worried that refusal might get her real prescription withdrawn, agreed.

She'd had no intention of baking, but once home she remembered how she'd responded to the doctor saying she needed more than the prescription drugs. She'd known it was true, and she had promised to try the cake. She couldn't very well ask for something a bit more scientific without making some kind of effort to do as she'd been urged. At least it wasn't the trite suggestions of going for a walk, spending time outside or taking part in social activities, which people seemed to think would magically solve all her problems.

Baking wasn't something Aiofe had ever done much of, and she didn't have all the ingredients. It would be easier to buy a beautifully iced, plastic wrapped confection, which promised so much and delivered nothing but calories. How long had it been since she'd had a slice of real cake?

Aiofe picked up her car keys, then remembered the parking situation in the village and decided to walk. Three people said hello to her – more than she'd spoken to in… forever it seemed.

The lady in the shop, Sue, seemed pleased to see Aiofe. Of course customers were always welcome in small businesses, but it didn't feel as cynical as that.

"Making a cake?" Sue asked, as Aiofe put the ingredients on the counter.

"Yes."

"A special occasion is it?"

"No… I just fancied homemade cake." That was sort of true.

"Good for you! Well, enjoy it."

"Thanks, I'm sure I will." As Aiofe spoke, that feeling she'd noticed in the doctor's surgery grew stronger. She'd felt like that before, hadn't she?

Aiofe weighed everything out, switched on the oven and greased the tin, just as directed. As she creamed together the stated quantities of butter and sugar, she realised the cake was going to be a large one. As she sifted the flour and beat the eggs she thought maybe that didn't matter. As the delicious aroma of baking cake filled her kitchen, Aiofe knew it was a good thing. She picked up her phone and dialled once familiar numbers.

By the time the cake had cooled, been sandwiched together with rich plum jam and lightly dusted with icing sugar, people began to arrive. Aiofe's sister was first, then her kindly neighbour and all the friend's she'd ignored, pushed away, thought were better off without her. They drank tea, ate cake and were there for her. Just as they always would have been if she'd let them.

That afternoon happiness bubbled through Aiofe – the first hints of which she'd felt as the new doctor had smiled at her, and offered fresh hope. Life for Aiofe wasn't uniformly wonderful after that. Her mood often crashed – but didn't sink quite so low as it had once been. Not so low that she couldn't make herself go out for a walk, bake a cake, or pick up the phone and talk to those people who cared about her happiness.

6. Speaking Of Bullies

Sarah half recognised the woman standing outside the hall. It wasn't familiar features which had her walking over with a friendly smile, but the woman's posture and the way she picked at the strap of her bag. The woman was nervous. Scared even.

Sarah had felt that way often enough to feel instant sympathy. And to have a good idea about how to help. "Hi," she called. As Sarah walked over, she saw the other woman studying her, trying to work out if she knew her.

"Thanks for waiting," Sarah said once she was close enough not to need to shout. "I'm Sarah and I'm so pleased not everyone has gone in yet. I didn't like the idea of making a grand entrance all on my own. May I walk in with you?" She was conscious of her words tumbling out in a rush, but thought she'd made enough sense to get her message across.

"Um, yes… I suppose."

As Sarah reached the other woman, she saw a thick ribbon leading to a name badge tucked into her breast pocket. The nerves instantly made sense – Mrs T Williams must be one of the speakers.

"Oh, wow!" Sarah said, her voice full of admiration. "Bullying is something I feel strongly about, and it's so important to bring it into the open, let people know they're not alone. Even so, I've never talked about it publicly. It's great that you're doing this." Once again she rushed through what she was saying. She often did when it was anything personal, or for which she was unprepared.

"I'm not sure I'm going to be able to," the woman said. "I thought I could and went and signed in, but when they gave me this," she waved her name badge. "It all seemed so real. I had to come outside for a bit of fresh air."

"Oh. Yes, I can see it must be difficult."

"It's more than that. I'm not due to talk until the end, and I'm a wreck already."

Realising that sounding nervous herself wasn't going to help Mrs Williams, Sarah took a moment to control her breathing. Hoping distraction would help she said, "I thought it might rain tonight."

The other woman glanced up. "Can't see any clouds."

"Guess that's why it's so cold. It often is on clear nights. Let's go inside."

Mrs Williams turned slightly, as though to go in, then shook her head. "I don't think I can."

"You don't need to speak. We could sit at the back and listen for a bit, and you could see how you feel then."

"If I hide at the back they'll think I left, and there's no way I'll jump up and interrupt to say I'm there and then have to squeeze through the crowd to reach the stage."

"No, I suppose not," Sarah conceded.

"And if I go in wearing this," she waved her name badge, "they'll assume I'm speaking and send me down the front. Then it'll be really hard to get out of it."

Sarah hadn't meant to trick her that way, but saw Mrs Williams was probably right. She also knew that if she walked away this time, she was unlikely to find the confidence to try again anytime soon. Fading into the background, even disappearing completely, was an easy habit to develop and one which became increasingly hard to break.

"I know the thought of it is scary, but I'm sure it would be OK once you got started," Sarah coaxed.

"Easy for you to say. It won't be you up on the stage looking into a sea of faces."

"True," Sarah agreed. "Easy to say, not so easy to do, but I really have. For years I was too timid to speak up for myself, in meetings, or anywhere much, but with support from friends and colleagues I've overcome that. I've given presentations at work, to crowds as big as this one is likely to be. I still get nervous beforehand, but like I say, once I've started I'm OK."

The other woman looked sceptical. "Just because you got over a few nerves, it doesn't mean I can stand up and tell all those people …" She trailed off, looking more worried than ever.

"It was more than a few nerves. At school I was bullied so bad I came in an hour early so I could get to my tutor room without incident. I hid every break time, or found a way to stay with a teacher. Never spoke unless …"

"Stop!" Mrs Williams looked pale.

"Sorry, I didn't mean to bring back bad memories." Sarah gently touched the woman's arm. "I have, haven't I?"

Mrs Williams nodded.

"I really am sorry. I was just trying to show people can change. At one time I'd never have walked up to a stranger and started talking, but when I saw you …"

"You didn't ask me to walk in with you because you're nervous, did you? It's because you could see I was?"

Sarah nodded. "Yeah. Not that I won't be glad of your company, but I no longer need a friend by my side in order to face a crowd, or speak my mind."

"I can see that. I'm glad of that, but… You said you had support? I won't."

"You will. You do. I'll be right there, eager to hear what you have to say. So will everyone in there. They'll all be on your side."

"I very much doubt that."

"One thing I've found helpful is to… Hey, it's OK, you don't have to do this if you really don't want to. Everyone will understand. Tell you what, I could read your speech for you." Sarah would still find it difficult to publicly discuss details of the bullying she'd received, but she could definitely read someone else's words – and hearing them and witnessing the reaction should make Mrs Williams feel better about not being able to speak herself.

"You?"

"Yes."

"You, who were terrorised by a school bully will read this?" She opened her bag, pulled out some papers and shoved them at Sarah.

Sarah read the opening lines. *Hello, I'm Tanya Williams and I'm here to talk about school bullying from a very different point of view. I was involved in many cruel incidents, but never as the victim.*

"I thought I recognised you," a very shocked Sarah whispered.

Tanya too spoke quietly. "I'm ashamed to say I don't have a clue who you are. I ruined your life and forgot you."

In the silence which followed, Sarah skimmed through Tanya's speech. She admitted being a bully and apologised. Without excusing her actions, she tried to explain them, in the hope that would be of help to those trying to prevent others behaving as badly.

Without asking for sympathy she stated that everyone involved with bullying was eventually a victim. In some cases, the bullies were plagued with remorse, in others they continued to be horrible people, but that too had a negative impact on their lives. It was, of course, worse for the victims, but for all of them the effects would last a lifetime.

"You're wrong," Sarah said gently. "In some ways at least. When I said I thought I recognised you, it was in a general sense, as someone who'd suffered as I had. Now I see that's true in a way. And although someone like you made me miserable for a time, I'm fine now."

"Really?" Tanya asked.

"Yes, really. But I still think people need to hear this. Not everyone recovers as I have. Your apology might help some, and hearing why you acted as you did might help others."

"That's why I said I'd do it, but I still don't think I can."

"You can. Like I said, everyone in there will be eager to hear what you have to say and I'll be right there by your side."

Tanya gave a tiny smile. "That's not exactly what you said."

"Maybe not, but it's what's going to happen. Deal?" Sarah held out her hand.

"Deal." Tanya shook Sarah's outstretched hand, then walked towards the hall.

As they reached the glass doors, Sarah saw their reflections. She recognised the nervous expression on Tanya's face, saw it fade and be replaced with her own friendly smile, as she followed her in.

7. Lizzie Wells Really Smells

"Lizzie Wells really smells, Lizzie Wells really smells," the girls chant as Lizzie queues up for her school lunch. "Whiffy Lizzie makes me dizzy," follows her down the corridor and into the canteen.

She pretends she hasn't heard them. Just like her mum told her. "Don't give them the satisfaction of knowing they're getting to you. They'll get fed up in the end."

They hadn't though and to make matters worse Lizzie's best friend Cheryl had moved away. With no one else to talk to during break times it was getting harder for Lizzie to ignore the taunts.

Lizzie piled curry and chips onto her plate, picked up a slice of treacle tart and a can of coke and looked around for an empty table. She'd learnt not to try and sit near her class mates. If she did, they would pretend to be sick, or complain her BO would curdle their custard. There were very few spaces, so Lizzie sat on a table with some older boys. They didn't know her, so might leave her alone. Soon the boys began to sniff and ask each other, "Was that you?"

Now the boys were doing it too. Lizzie had no friends and it didn't seem likely she'd ever get a boyfriend either. No one liked her, they wouldn't talk to her, or even let her sit next to them if they had a choice.

Lizzie began to sweat. She couldn't help it. Whenever she got upset she'd begin sweating. Her face and armpits felt as though water was running off them, her feet and hands were damp too. It was so bad she thought she might lose her grip on her fork. Lizzie concentrated on eating her food as quickly as possible. It didn't seem to help.

Back outside the chants started up again.

With, "Lizzie Wells really smells, Lizzie Wells really smells," ringing in her ears she went early to her next lesson. At least in the classroom she was free from the nasty comments around her.

Lizzie had only been in the room for a few minutes when her teacher arrived. "Hello, Lizzie, you're early."

"Yes, Miss."

"It's warm today, isn't it? I think I'll just open a window at let some fresh air in."

Surely Miss Evans wasn't siding with the bullies! It just wasn't fair. Lizzie started to cry.

"Hey, Lizzie, what's the matter?" Miss Evans asked.

Lizzie could tell her teacher was concerned. "Some of the girls have been calling me names. They say I smell."

"Oh dear. Well, that's not very nice is it?"

"No, Miss. My Mum says I should just ignore them, but I can't."

"Does your mum know what they say?"

"Not really."

"I think perhaps you should tell her."

When Lizzie got home, she did as Miss Evans had suggested.

"Why do they say it, Mum?"

"Because they're nasty bullies, that's why. It's not fair to tease someone for something they can't help."

"Do you mean my sweating? I remember you told me it's a medical condition, focal hypo something."

"That's right. Focal Hyperhidrosis the name is. I know about it because your Aunty Cynthia told me. She's got it, and her son and your granddad."

At the start of half term, Lizzie's mum rang and told Aunty Cynthia that Lizzie was being teased and her aunty came to talk to her about it.

"Lizzie, you know I love you right?"

"Yes, Aunty Cynthia."

"Then you'll know I'm not being unkind when I ask you to have a shower."

"You think I smell too?"

"Yes, Lizzie, I'm afraid so. Now go and have that shower and I'll tell you how to get this sorted."

"It won't help much. Nothing does."

"What soap and antiperspirant do you use, Lizzie?"

"I don't, my skin's too sore."

"I thought as much. Here use this to wash with, then borrow your mum's antiperspirant."

Lizzie took her shower and used the emollient cream her aunt had given her to wash with. She sprayed herself with Mum's body spray afterwards. She took the spray downstairs. "Will this really help?"

"No, that one won't. What you need is antiperspirant, that helps stop the sweating. All this stuff will do is mask the smell."

"That's good isn't it?"

"No, Lizzie. You need to stop the smell from happening in the first place."

"How?"

"Well, by using the antiperspirant. We'll get you some from the chemist. If it's not strong enough you can get Aluminium chloride, but try the regular stuff first; the strong one can irritate your skin. It's not the sweat that smells though, Lizzie. It's when it goes stale or gets on your clothes. You'll need to have a clean blouse and socks every morning, then change when you come in from school."

"And will that stop me getting teased?"

"It will help. It would be a good idea to get some new clothes. You've grown a bit recently and things are tight. Loose clothes would be better and read the label; get cotton, not nylon."

"Anything else?"

"Try wearing different shoes on alternate days, so they dry out. Try to avoid spicy foods, that can make it worse."

"It's all a lot of fuss isn't it?"

"A bit, but it's nothing too serious and you really don't want to smell do you?"

"No, you're right. Will I grow out of it? Or will I just get worse?"

"Neither. It's likely to stay the same. You're lucky, some people have it all over, or they get it much worse than you and need treatment – your grandad did."

Lizzie and her mum went shopping. They bought some mild soap and antiperspirant. They asked the chemist for advice and where told that the aluminium chloride could be bought without prescription if it was needed. Lizzie bought new cotton blouses for school and some loose tops to change into. They bought dark colours which wouldn't show sweat marks, just in case Lizzie sweated more than usual.

When Lizzie went back to school she hadn't even got inside the gates before she heard the chants,

"Lizzie Wells really smells, Lizzie Wells really smells."

Lizzie walked up to the group. She had showered less than an hour ago, applied the antiperspirant and put on a brand new blouse. For the first time in months, she felt confident. "No, actually I don't. I used to, but I don't anymore."

After that, no one mentioned that she smelt until the end of term prom. One of the sixth form boys asked her to dance. He lead her onto the floor and put his arm around her waist. As he drew her close he said, "You smell really nice, Lizzie."

8. Driven To Doubt

I think of the day my pregnancy was confirmed; it's hard to believe I'm the same woman. Sunk into the soft cream sofa, I'd daydreamed of my future. With hands placed over my still flat belly, I'd thought I could already feel the new life growing there. I imagined walking my child to school, watching him in school plays, sticking his pictures onto the fridge.

Smiling complacently to myself, I considered my soon to be promoted husband – he'd told me there were to be changes in the company. When I asked if they'd make him a director he told me not to get my hopes up. He's so modest. How smug we would be at dinner parties, with our perfect lifestyle, perfect marriage and perfect child.

We'd spent all of our savings on fertility treatment but Chris had a good job and promotion would mean more money still. I was to work until the last possible moment, although I would not be returning to work after the birth. We have invested a great deal of time, emotion, and money too, although that isn't important. It's unlikely I will conceive again so this child is extra precious.

Everything was fine at first. Our families were thrilled for us and Chris and I were ecstatic. If anything, Chris had been the more pleased.

"A dad! Oh, Annie I'm going to be a dad. I'll be the best dad in the world, that kid will want for nothing." He'd leapt around the room, childlike himself, in his joyful excitement.

"Of course not. He won't have to survive on welfare and dress in hand-me-downs like I did," I agreed.

"Oh love, I didn't mean to criticise your family. Your parents did the best they could. It wasn't your dad's fault he lost his job. He took any work he could get, didn't he? And they really loved you and your sister. That's what matters isn't it?"

"Of course it is and it's not as if we starved. It must have been really hard for them both though. I just hope I'll be as good a mum."

Only a month into the pregnancy my blood pressure began to rise. I needed regular monitoring. The doctors assured me that although an early delivery was likely there was every reason to hope I would have a healthy baby.

I still went to work but no longer dealt with difficult clients. Chris did all he could to pamper me and keep me away from any form of stress. He dealt with all the household accounts and running of our home.

Five months before the baby was due, he came home early from work very, very, drunk. He was angry. I've never known him to lose his temper and this was much more than that. He ranted round the house yelling things that made no sense. He smashed several ornaments and treasured holiday souvenirs. I was terrified. I really believed he might hit me. I ran to the neighbours, fearful any injury to me would result in the loss of our child. Sally tried to comfort me and her husband tried to reason with Chris. Much later he came back and reported Chris was now asleep or possibly passed out. He didn't like to leave him alone, so he spent the night at our house and I stayed with Sally.

The next day Chris was extremely depressed. I put this down to a combination of guilt and a hangover. He said he didn't want to talk about it and remembering how angry he'd been I didn't push it.

Quietly we cleared up the mess, then Chris went out for a walk. He took nothing with him not even his wallet. He'd been gone six hours and I'd called everyone I could think of and was actually looking through the yellow pages for the number of the police station when he came home. He seemed to have no idea where he'd been or for how long. He ate his supper but it was obvious he hardly realised he was doing so.

The rest of the week passed like that. He didn't go to work just sat around the house or went for long walks. I tried to get him to talk to me. The closest I got to an explanation was a yelled, "I HAD A BAD DAY."

I tried to cheer him up by talking about the baby and the marvellous future we had. That clearly made him more depressed.

I didn't know who to turn to as I'd not told anyone about the drunken outburst. This was partly because I knew how ashamed Chris would be, but also I got so upset thinking about it, I thought I could harm our precious baby.

The following week Sally came round whilst Chris was on one of his walks.

"I'm not trying to pry. What happened that night was between you and your husband. I just wanted to say if you want someone to talk to, well I'm only next door. Sometimes it's easier to speak to someone who isn't involved. And as I know some of what happened, and how out of character it was, you wouldn't have a lot of explaining to do."

"Thanks, Sally. That's kind. Thanks too for Tuesday. I'm sorry I haven't been round to thank you. Guess I've been too embarrassed."

"It's OK. All I did was make a few cups of tea. The guest room is always ready so it wasn't any trouble."

Alone, I lie again on our soft cream sofa but now my unconscious thoughts have more of a nightmare quality. Daydreams belong to the old me.

I can smell smoke on Chris's clothes. I'm positive I can, or nearly positive.

"Oh don't start again, Annie we've been through it all before. Can't a man even walk through his front door without being interrogated?"

Maybe I am a bit on edge, but I'm not the only one. He never used to raise his voice or shout at me. If he's been somewhere smoky why can't he just say so? I'm not accusing him of anything. He doesn't have to take offence every time I make a simple comment. That's probably why we speak so little. It's safer to say nothing and just keep those little doubts, quietly niggling, at the back of my mind.

When he says he's working late I don't say anything. I just accept it when he claims to have been sent away on weekend courses. I try not to question him when I'm told he's staying the night at his friend's home after a drink with the lads. I don't really believe any of it, but living with doubt seems preferable to having my fears confirmed. Then he'll be home for a few days, time off to compensate for the late nights and weekends away. He's happy then, loving and attentive. My doubts disappear. I love him so much and know he loves me too. When I ask about his hours becoming more flexible after the rigid nine to five regime, he shrugs. Muttering about work changes and re-alignments. He doesn't like to talk about it. One more thing we don't discuss.

Seven years we've been married and I've never before doubted his love or loyalty. Perhaps that's what's troubling me? Some silly superstition of the seven year itch. Could it just be the effects of the pregnancy? That's what he'd said when I thought I could smell a women's perfume on him. That I was imagining it. The hormones were affecting my sense of smell. It was just his usual aftershave.

Come to think of it he was a bit defensive. I hadn't thought anything of it, except that maybe someone in the office had been spraying it about. I'd half hoped he'd been sprayed in a shop whilst buying a gift for me. He often used to surprise me with little presents. That stopped recently. Just as my belly began to swell.

Whenever I had doubts about Chris's behaviour I'd talk it over with Sally. She never judged us or told me what to do. Over the next few weeks I was often round at Sally's. Life with Chris settled back into a routine of sorts. We were happy, although I always felt he was keeping something back. He never spoke about work. Before he was always telling me amusing stories about colleagues or having a quiet moan if things didn't go well.

I knew there were things he didn't talk to me about. Things he didn't want me to notice. Friends would mention seeing him when I knew he'd been at work. I agreed with Chris that our mates were easily confused, especially after a pint or nine. When an attractive, scantily clad, girl thanked him for getting her safely home last Saturday I agreed with Chris about everyone having a double. If I phoned my family for a chat he got angry, reminding me about the cost of calling long distance. I felt he was trying to cut me off from the rest of the world. It was as if now I was to be the mother of his child I was no longer a person in my own right.

I waddle next door, seeking reassurance. Sally says maybe he's just worried over money. Why should he be though? We'd gone through our finances carefully when we'd begun to seek help in conceiving this child. We aren't rich by any means but a pound or two for a phone call surely isn't a problem. It feels like everyone is siding against me. Sally defends Chris, telling me life is unsettling for him at the moment; that he has things to worry about.

"Like what? I'm the one who's pregnant. My body is changing, not his. I'm the one whose life will change forever."

"And how is it easier for Chris?"

"Nothing ever changes in his safe little world."

"Is that right?"

"You know it is. He'll carry on in his cushy office job; keeping his friends and social life. Maybe if I'm lucky he might bother to visit me in hospital, if he can spare the time. If he wants to spend time with his child he'll have to give up an evening in the pub with his mates but maybe he will think the baby worth the sacrifice even if I'm not."

"Is that really what you think he's doing; sitting down the pub?"

"Of course he is. There's always money for that isn't there? But when I said I wanted to decorate the nursery he claimed we can't afford it, he hasn't got the time and there's no point anyway as the baby won't appreciate it. What about me? Don't I matter?"

"You ungrateful cow! He's working himself into exhaustion to pay the bills and you just nag him about luxuries."

"Luxuries! It's over a month since I had my hair or nails done, yet he's just gone out and bought an expensive car and I reckon he must have had an accident in the old one and not told me because I saw the insurance cost and it's ridiculous."

"It would be more expensive than for an ordinary car wouldn't it?"

"Sally!" her husband interrupts her. I'm so upset I hadn't even realised he was home.

"It's time she knew the truth, Dave."

"We promised Chris we wouldn't say anything."

"Because we thought it would help. Well, it isn't working. Look at the state she's got herself into. She's imagining all kinds of things. The baby is due very soon. If she knows the truth she'll be able to make sensible choices for the future."

"What are you talking about? Dave tell me. Is Chris going to leave me when I have the baby?"

"You're right Sal, the truth would be better than this."

"Dave, tell me, he's talked to you hasn't he?" Dave just looks embarrassed. He shrugs his shoulders, kisses his wife, and leaves the room.

"So, Sally, you know what my lousy husband is up to and have been keeping it from me? Great friend you are." And she called me an ungrateful cow. She had said that, hadn't she? I'm beginning to doubt what's real, and what might be my hormone overloaded 'baby brain' imaging all kinds of unpleasant things. Please let it just be that.

"Annie, I thought it was for the best, honestly I did. Chris promised he'd tell you the truth as soon as the baby was born. He didn't want to tell you before as he didn't want to worry you."

"Didn't work – I'm worried."

"Yeah, I got that."

"So, tell me now," I beg.

"I don't know where to start."

I'm so agitated my whole body is shaking and I hurt. Great fingers of distress are squeezing my belly. I hear a woman screaming, swearing, demanding to know the truth. I'm only half aware it's me. I try to regain control of myself, and say more calmly, "Just tell me. Stop lying and stalling, if you care about me at all just tell me the truth. All of it. Now."

"I still think it would be better if he told you himself, perhaps we can get him here."

I'm so angry I can hear my heart racing; my pain is physical as well as emotional. Time after time, waves of grief and tension grip my body in angry spasms, making it difficult to speak.

"Dave, can you see if you can get hold of Chris?" Sally shrieks at her husband, the panic in her voice only adding to mine. When I can speak I ask her to explain, pleading with her. Only the truth will ease the pain, give me back self control.

"The car, why did he change the car?" I ask. Sally had spoken of that as though it were the logical thing for him to do.

"He had to have a new one, that old Citroen wasn't going to impress anyone was it?"

"Who the hell did he need to impress?"

"It could be anyone, whoever he picked up."

Nothing makes sense. Her tone and manner say she's comforting me; her words suggest my husband is out picking up strange women. That woman is screaming again. The woman I know is me. Maybe I really am mad.

"His colleagues from work. Why don't I see them? Why doesn't he talk about them?"

"He doesn't really know them; he hardly sees them at all."

"Of course he does, he's always with them. They used to come round for dinner parties. Chris won't let me invite them any more, and they never invite us."

"You mean the people from the office?"

"Who the hell else would I mean?"

"I don't think Chris wants anything to do with them now. I don't suppose they do either, embarrassed to see him probably."

"Why? What has he done?"

"Look it wasn't his fault, it was bound to happen."

"Bound to! That sort of thing isn't happening to me."

"You're pregnant and will be leaving work soon anyway. He's young and talented. He'll soon find something else."

"So that's it? I'm fat and pregnant so he's quite justified in having affairs."

"Don't be silly I never said that."

"And he's a bright attractive man who doesn't need to be saddled with a wife and kid. He'll soon find a replacement for me."

"No!"

"Too right he won't, I'll see to it. He wanted this baby too, you know."

"Of course he did. Does. You know what I mean. He loves you. You aren't thinking straight."

"Stop talking rubbish then. If he loves me why's he having affairs? Why am I all wet? Oh God help me, Sally. What the hell is happening to me?"

"DAVE! Have you got hold of Chris yet?"

"No but I've left a message. They said they would send him straight round."

I scream again. I'm so frightened, my whole world has disappeared into pain and confusion.

"There's no time. Get an ambulance, a taxi, anything. Annie has to get to hospital. Now."

"Hospital? Sally what's happening?"

"You're in labour you silly cow. Oh God you hadn't realised! No wonder you're so scared and haven't been concentrating."

"Labour? My baby will he be ok?"

"Of course he will,. Try to relax, we'll get you to hospital. Chris knows, he'll be with you soon."

"If he wants me now."

"Of course he does. I told you, he loves you."

"I know you did, but I still don't understand. I need him with me." Not all my doubts have gone, but I know I still love him – and Sally sounds so sure about him loving me.

And we'll have a baby very soon now. The joy of that thought pushes out some of my worry.

I begin to calm down as Sally again explains about Chris. The contractions hurt of course, but they don't terrify me now. I'm looking forward to having my child to hold. I begin to realise I wasn't the only one who'd been through changes during the pregnancy. I realised some of the rows have been partly my fault. I've been too quick to judge Chris. I haven't been a very supportive wife and I've added to his problems. It isn't entirely my fault. I hadn't asked him to lie to me.

My thoughts are interrupted by Dave. "He's here."

Sally and Dave between them help me out of the house, towards the waiting taxi. As we travel to the hospital I try to make sense of what I've learnt. Chris had lost his job. Those changes I'd so confidently assumed meant he'd gain a promotion had worked against him. He'd not had the heart to tell me, and worried he would lose me and the baby too, if he couldn't support us.

Things begin to make sense; his unhappiness and the secrecy. Losing his job explains why there have been no gifts or nights out. He couldn't afford them. I've misjudged my husband. I've not lost him though – he's there holding my hand as I give birth to our beautiful daughter, Heather Florence (after her grandmothers).

As she sleeps we talk and talk. I learn that after losing his job, Chris had started taxi driving. He'd not wanted to concern me as I was already so anxious about the baby. Alone he'd shouldered all the worry, begun to build up a business.

"I'm doing really well, Annie love. I've got regular clients now and sometimes have to turn down bookings. With your support, we could expand – take on other drivers."

"Of course I'll help. I can do the paperwork and take bookings from home." I'm tired, but so happy. Our little family has a future. It isn't the one I'd imagined, but I'm done with imagining the worst. I'm looking forward to the future with hope.

9. The Big One

"What'll you spend the money on if we win the big one, Jen?" Lorraine asked her friend as they waited for the bingo to start. The women had an agreement to split all their prize money.

"You know what, you ask me every week."

"I keep hoping you'll come up with something more exciting than new carpets."

"I'd like new carpets, Raine," Jenny said.

"Yeah, but they're not very exciting are they? I'd go travelling."

"Yes, I know you would. Where to this time?"

Although Lorraine had never won 'the big one' she had been on a couple of foreign holidays and had planned several hundred trips.

"Well, you know how I can never decide where would be best?"

"Yes." Jenny had listened to hours of debate over the merits of an assortment of potential travel destinations.

"I've worked it out – I'm going on a round the world cruise!" Lorraine lifted her half of lager and lime and took a swig as if to toast the wisdom of her decision.

"Oooh, that does sound nice. If I was to go away, it'd be on a cruise."

"Thought you didn't want to go abroad?" Lorraine asked. Since they'd agreed to split their winnings, Lorraine had hoped to persuade her friend that the money should be spent on a holiday together. So far, Jenny had been unimpressed by every exotic location Lorraine had suggested.

"It's not the holiday I don't like the idea of; it's the flying. I worry I'd get that deep vein thrombosis stuff or that I'd be ill without my medicine. I have to take pills all the time, you know."

"Yes, you said, but where's the problem? Just make sure you take enough with you. I take pills too, and I just make sure I take all I'll need plus a couple extra in case there's a delay or anything."

"Don't they search you for drugs? You might get arrested," Jenny asked.

"No, you wally! It's only illegal drugs that can get you into trouble. Prescription stuff and things you buy over the counter are OK. What I do is carry them in my handbag, with all the proper packaging and I take a copy of the repeat prescription form, too. That way they can tell what it is and if I was to loose them or anything, I'd be able to show a doctor wherever I went and they'd know exactly what I'd need."

The bingo caller picked up the microphone and their conversation stopped until the first prize was claimed.

"You're right that a cruise would be best," Lorraine said as though the holiday had been Jenny's idea.

"Hmm, I don't know, Raine. Don't you get all kinds of stomach bug on ships?"

"Not always. Sometimes people do, but they could get a bug at home. As long as everyone washes their hands after going to the loo and before eating and drinking, then they won't catch anything or pass it on if they've got it. The ships have special cleaning gel in all the restaurants too. They take care to try and keep people healthy."

Lorraine knew all this as she always studied the whole brochure, including the healthcare advice. She asked her pharmacist for advice before travelling and read all the 'useful information for travellers' leaflets she found both in the pharmacy and at her local health centre. Her holiday time was far too precious to waste on being ill, especially if the illness was avoidable.

"I suppose so. It just gets in the papers don't it? If it's on a ship. I bet just as many people get dodgy stomachs on other holidays."

"Probably. From what I've seen it's because they eat too much food they're not used to and drink too much alcohol and don't take proper care. In some countries it's best not to drink the tap water or even have ice made from it. You also want to eat food that's freshly made – not been kept warm for hours on end."

Another game began and the women kept their eyes down and mouths shut. After another prize had been won by someone else, Jenny fetched a round of drinks. As she sat next to her friend, a fly buzzed around her. She batted it away with her free hand.

"Good thing you're not abroad yet, or that could be a mosquito," Lorraine said. "If you go anywhere they have them, you'll need tablets to stop you getting malaria if they bite you."

"I'd rather nothing bit me in the first place."

"Yeah, me too. I'd wear insect repellent and get one of those things you burn in your room to scare them away."

Jenny nodded her agreement. "Raine, I was thinking about people who're already ill before they go away, or are disabled or something. Can they still go on holiday? I suppose they can?"

"If it was something contagious like the stomach bugs we were on about then it'd be best not to, wouldn't it? With lots of people shut up together on a plane or ship then it wouldn't be fair in case you passed it on. You'd have to claim on their insurance and go later instead."

"You'd need insurance then, you reckon?" Jenny asked.

"Yeah. You have to if you go abroad. It's only sensible to make sure that you could pay for emergency treatment if you did need it. Accidents and things can happen even if you're careful and treatment can be very expensive. Of course, getting the money back isn't as good as not getting ill or injured to start with. People have to be as sensible as they would at home."

"How d'you mean?"

"Well, if they can't ride a moped in England then they can't expect to ride one safely on roads they don't know or to be safe doing it in flip flops and shorts. Or if they go for a drink they shouldn't have twice as much just 'cos it's cheap and then try and find their way home along cliff tops in the dark."

"Yeah, I see what you mean. A bit of common sense never goes amiss does it?"

"Exactly, Jen. Same if you have a medical condition. It'd make sense to check with your doctor if you're not sure if you should travel. If it was me, I'd tell the holiday company too, especially if I needed a special diet or help getting around or anything. If they know in plenty of time then they should be able to help. Do you know, they can even supply oxygen for people in their cabins on cruise ships?"

"That's good, but what if you're not staying in a classy hotel or on a cruise ship?"

"If anyone needed special equipment or was going somewhere they thought they wouldn't get good medical treatment, then they'd have to take stuff with them. Say, if you were going to stay in a jungle for a month, you'd need a better first aid kit than for a week on a beach."

"That makes sense. I hope anyone doing anything adventurous would know to be extra careful."

During the third game, Jenny got every number one after the other until she only needed one more. It was never called.

"My round," Lorraine said.

"So, if I did go, would I need injections and things beforehand?" Jenny asked as she accepted her drink.

"Maybe, it would depend where we went. The health centre can give the answer to that or the pharmacy or we could look it up on the internet. No problem. So you're thinking about it? We could see the snowy fjords first, then sail out to Caribbean beaches and …"

"Hold you horses. You've not convinced me yet. What if I get sea sick?"

"We'll get you some pills. If you think it's likely we'll go to the chemist and ask for advice. While we're there we can put together a simple first aid kit."

"Oh? You're going to play doctor are you?"

"No, you w…"

"Don't call me a wally again, Rain, or I'm definitely not coming."

"As I was saying… no, you wonderful person. I was thinking of plasters, painkillers and antiseptic, stuff like that. Just the kind of thing we'd have at home."

Jenny didn't answer, because the final game – 'the big one' was about to begin and she didn't want to be distracted.

"OK, you win," she said a few minutes later.

"I flippin' well haven't!"

"Not the bingo, you, what is it? Oh yes, 'wonderful person'. You've convinced me. If we win any money, we'll spend it on a trip."

"Brilliant!"

As usual, Jenny and Lorraine ended the evening by putting a pound each into the one armed bandit. Jenny won £50. "Fair do, I'm sticking to our deal. Half each. Shame it's not enough for a cruise."

"How about a day trip to the Isle of Wight?"

"You don't give up do you, Raine?"

"You know me so well, Jen! You will come, won't you? Oh go on, say yes."

"All right then. It might be fun."

"It will, I promise and at least we won't need to worry about medical precautions."

"Yes we will. I'm surprised at you, Raine, you being such a seasoned traveller! You forget that even if you're not going abroad you still need to take care."

"All right, I'll bring an aspirin. Anything else?"

"We'll need plenty of suntan lotion. Just because it's not the Caribbean doesn't mean we won't get burned."

"OK, sounds sensible. While you're in the pharmacy, I'm going to call into the travel agents and pick up some brochures."

"For a day trip? That's taking planning a bit far!" Jenny said.

"No, you w… What I mean is we'll start getting ideas of where we're going when we win the big one."

10. Sisterly Unity

The whole time Ailsa had been deadheading roses and watering the hanging baskets, a delicious smell of baking had wafted out from the kitchen. When she came in she discovered her daughter Fi had baked and iced a gorgeous rainbow cake.

"I haven't forgotten someone's birthday, have I?" Ailsa asked.

"No – don't panic!" Fi laughed, as she carried it to the pantry.

It was a standing joke that Ailsa jumped to wrong conclusions and imagined disasters on the flimsiest of evidence.

"It's a surprise to congratulate Kiera on passing her driving test," Fi explained.

Yesterday, Ailsa had seen her younger daughter returning from the test in the passenger seat of the instructor's car, and been ready to commiserate, only for Kiera to leap out yelling, "I did it!"

As Kiera was upstairs studying and Ailsa had smelled the cake from the garden, there wasn't going to be much surprise, but it was a lovely gesture. "Your sister will love it," Ailsa assured her.

Fi's phone, left out on the kitchen table, rang.

Ailsa seeing 'Shona' on the caller ID, immediately plunged her hands into the sink full of soapy water, where Fi had put the cake tin and icing equipment to soak. She'd much rather wash up than speak to her own sister.

Unlike Fi and Kiera, Ailsa and Shona didn't get on. There wasn't much over a year between them and as kids they were often mistaken for twins. They were treated that way too and expected to share everything. If Mum could scrape together a little spare money for sweets, it was always a big bar of chocolate or bag of toffees between them, not a smaller one each.

If a friend invited them for tea, or one wanted to join Brownies, Mum would agree for both or neither – then worked extra hours while they were out. She insisted on a show of sisterly unity and that they never complain of the other in her hearing. They resented that so much it had the opposite result to that which Mum intended.

Ailsa hadn't repeated the mistake with her daughters. Fi and Kiera were individuals with their own friends and interests, and loved each other dearly.

"Kiera," Fi called now, as she raced upstairs. "I know you're busy, but it's urgent." She sounded flustered.

Ailsa hadn't spoken to Shona in quite a while, but if she discovered her sister had said something to upset her kids, she'd be having words with her! She went into the hallway.

"What's up?" Kiera called out.

"Aunty Shona's in hospital and doesn't have much time left."

Ailsa was abruptly taken back to hearing almost exactly the same thing, two years previously. The only differences were that it was Shona who'd been speaking, and she'd been talking about their mum.

Ailsa and Shona had sat by her bedside and held a hand each as she slipped away. Afterwards they'd hugged and sobbed. They comforted each other as they'd organised the funeral and laid Mum to rest.

Then the bickering started. Not over money, there wasn't much and it was easily divided. Mum, of course, had left her few pieces of jewellery and personal effects to 'my girls'. They'd both wanted to keep some, but neither had the stronger claim to any one piece. Ailsa loved the dragonfly brooch which had been Granny's, and wore it every chance she got, but Mum had insisted Shona borrow it just as frequently. It was the same story with every little trinket, and they'd argued over them all. Then, without Mum insisting they come together to visit and expecting to hear they'd shared important moments in the other's life, they'd stopped contacting each other at all.

It was over a year since they'd last spoken. Time enough to realise the arguments were due to the resentment they'd always felt at being one half of a pair, and the grief they'd both felt but been unable to share. Mum would have wanted them to comfort each other. Guilt they'd done the opposite was another wedge pushing them apart. Their stubbornness kept it in place, or had until now.

Now she was faced with losing her, Ailsa realised she loved her sister and always had. It was a shame they'd ever fallen out and stupid they'd continued the animosity into adulthood. Ailsa had been blaming Shona, but was just as much at fault herself.

Maybe it wasn't too late to put things right? It would take less than a minute to hug Shona and say sorry. She suddenly knew that was all she'd have to do.

If Ailsa went by train she could be there in three hours. She'd be in time, surely? It was worth trying, worth making the effort to patch things up with Shona.

"Kiera, Fi!" she called.

The girls raced down.

"I heard what you said… How long does she have?"

"Who, Mum?" Fi asked.

"Your aunt… Not long you said. Shona's in hospital and doesn't have long."

Her daughters exchanged glances, but didn't reply.

"Did she ask you not to tell me she's ill?"

"It's nothing like that, Mum," Kiera said.

"She didn't actually say …"

Kiera interrupted Fi with, "We agreed never to talk about you to her and vice versa, remember?"

Ailsa did. She'd not wanted them to feel their loyalties were torn and so suggested that. When she had, she learned Shona had formed the same plan. That they'd felt the same way proved something, didn't it?

"I was thinking… I might catch a train and go and see her. Do you think that's a good idea?"

"Yes," both girls agreed.

"Today?"

"I can take you to the station," Kiera offered. "You go and pack, Mum. I'll look up the train times."

Kiera accompanied Ailsa to her bedroom and helped select clothes. Fi called up to say the kettle was on and there was just time for a cuppa before Ailsa would have to go. She and Kiera hastily finished packing and went down.

As well as tea, the cake was on the table. Hearing Kiera's squeal of delight at the 'surprise' and seeing her daughters hug, confirmed Ailsa was doing the right thing in rushing to her own sister's bedside.

Fi wrapped a wedge of cake for Ailsa to eat on the journey as Kiera got the car out of the garage.

"You drink your tea, Mum. I'll put this in your case."

Kiera came in. "Car's ready. We'll call and make sure you're met at the station, Mum," she said. "So don't worry about that."

It was a rush getting the tickets and reaching the right platform and telling the girls to look after each other. Once on the train she phoned work. Her boss readily agreed to her taking the week off when she explained she was visiting her sick sister.

She'd missed a call from Fi, so rang her back.

"Mum… You know how you're always thinking the worst before you get all the facts?"

"I don't! Well, maybe sometimes… You mean Shona isn't as ill as I thought?"

"No, she isn't, but you'll still visit her, won't you?"

Given how relieved Ailsa felt, perhaps she should. "Will she want to see me?"

"She does, Mum. We've checked and your train is due in at seven twenty-three. You'll be picked up right outside the station."

"Thanks, love. Who is …"

"How's the cake?" Fi interrupted.

"I've not tried it yet. A refreshment trolley will be round — I'll get myself a coffee and have it then."

Ailsa decided to get it out ready, so her drink wouldn't get cold as she wrestled her case down from the shelf. Underneath the wrapped cake was a photo album. Not just any album, but one of two identical ones Mum once made up for her and Shona. Fi must have slipped it in.

Ailsa flipped through. Seeing the images of her sister smiling for the camera were bittersweet. Each one helped her recall incidents from their childhood. Not just times they were forced to be together or to share something, but also when they'd been pleased to do so. Yes, sometimes it had been irritating to have a constant shadow, but it had also been nice to have someone witness her every triumph and console her for every mini disaster. Mum's insistence that every treat and outing were shared meant they'd had more of both than would otherwise have been the case.

It didn't seem long before an announcement informed her she'd shortly be arriving at her destination. Waiting at the station was Shona.

Yes, it definitely was her sister and not Ailsa's imagination playing tricks. She didn't look at all sick, but of course you can't always tell.

Shona reached for Ailsa's case on wheels. "Let me take that."

"I can manage," Ailsa said.

"I didn't say you couldn't. Tell you what… we'll do it between us, eh?" She stood to one side and grasped the handle, so Ailsa could walk beside her and share the small amount of effort.

"Mum would have been pleased to see us like this," Ailsa ventured.

"She would… and even more pleased that I've made up the spare room for you and taken a few days off work."

"Oh! Um, thank you." She was glad Shona was well enough to work, but the last she'd heard, her sister had been made redundant.

"What's this about?" Shona asked. "Fi and Kiera say you're determined to make amends, but wouldn't explain the rush. I was relieved to see you looking well," Shona said. "I thought they meant …"

"I'm not sick, Sis. I thought you were," Ailsa said. "I'm really glad you're not."

"Same here," Shona said.

On the drive to Shona's home, Ailsa explained what she'd heard and why she'd reached the conclusion she had.

"I take it your girls hadn't told you about my new job as hospital porter?"

"You're right, they hadn't… I'm sure they didn't plan this. When I asked about you being ill Kiera said it was nothing like that, but when I suggested coming to see you, they encouraged me rather than saying I'd got it wrong. It sounds as though they might have given you room for misunderstanding too."

"Seems we were both very quick to react to the vague hint the other was seriously ill," Shona said.

"Yes, but not because we wanted it to be true. It's like when I thought Kiera had failed her driving test. I'd wanted her to pass of course, but I also wanted to show I loved her and was there for her no matter what."

"And I was looking for an excuse to mend bridges."

"How about we start again?" Ailsa suggested as they. "As sisters, but also two different people."

"I'd like that."

They hugged and spoke together, Shona saying, "I'm so glad you're here," and Ailsa saying. "I'm so glad I came."

The first thing Ailsa unpacked was the large wedge of cake. When she'd realised on the train that it was big enough to share with Shona she'd decided to do just that. Not because she had to, but because she wanted to. And she wanted to share memories with her sister – and make more.

11. Prickly Situation

"Sorry, but I really won't be able to make it to the party tonight, no matter how many fig leaves I wear," I said into Mandy's voice mail. I was dripping water onto the floor, because I'd just taken a cool shower to try and soothe my itchy skin and it occurred to me that she'd probably be showering too as part of her lengthy preparations for the evening out.

Yeah, I admit I deliberately timed the call to avoid talking to her. I know what she's like; there's no crisis on earth that she'd think was a reasonable excuse to avoid tonight's party. You see, Dishy Duncan is going to be there. Rumour has it that he'll be coming as a caveman. Did I mention that the party is fancy dress? I probably forgot to mention that Mandy fancies Duncan, but I expect you've guessed as much.

Mandy is a bit shy. Not with me, I wish she were sometimes, but she's not. She's shy about going into a room full of strangers though and she's shy around blokes she fancies. You can see why she wants me to come to the party with her, then. Especially when I tell you what she's going as: a lifeguard! You know, the Baywatch type, not the weirdos who hang out down the lido and throw rubber rings and poke you with hooks on sticks when you go under for the third time.

To sum up; shy Mandy really wants to go to the party, but she's not confident enough to go on her own. Normally, I'd be confident enough for the two of us; but not today. Not with this rash.

I was going to go as Eve. What it is, my brother works for a company who make props for stage plays. He came home the other day with a huge bag of plastic fig leaves. Yeah, weird I know; I thought it was just supposed to be businessmen who bring their work home with them, but apparently not. He brought home some other stuff too, including the scraps of fur he's going to wear. He's wearing the fur to the party, I should have said that. I wouldn't want you to think that Duncan's the kind of weirdo who normally wears nothing but leopard skin boxers to the club. Dishy Duncan is my brother—you are keeping up here aren't you? He's giving us a lift. Well, he would have done if I'd been going.

I'd have thought, and maybe you did too, that Mandy would have been happy that I wasn't going so she could have him all to herself without me as gooseberry. That's what I said when the rash first flared up. Did I tell you about the rash? I might not have as I don't like to go on, but as you asked, I'll explain. It's little red dots on my skin, in groups they are and they look like tiny blisters. I've got patches on different parts of my body. They're worst where my clothes touch. They don't exactly itch; it's more of an intense prickling sensation. Some of the skin is red. What I've got is Miliaria Rubra, or prickly heat to you and me.

This Miliaria thing is due to blocked sweat ducts. There are thousands of sweat glands just under the skin's surface. They make sweat which travels down the sweat duct to the skin's surface. If they're blocked, the sweat seeps into the skin. This causes tiny patches of inflammation which forms the rash.

Some people are more likely than others to get it. Bacteria called Staphylococcus epidermidis could be something to do with it. These bacteria live on the skin anyway; miliaria's not like an infection or anything. What happens is the bacteria make sticky stuff and that mixes with dead skin and sweat and that makes the blockage.

Bet you're surprised I know all this stuff, eh? I'll let you into the secret; I didn't until a while ago. I was thinking about wanting to go to the party, but not wanting to go with the rash, when Jezzer phoned to ask if I'd go with him. He keeps asking me out. He's really sweet to me, so I don't like to keep saying no, but he's a bit odd, so I don't often say yes either. Anyway, the rash gave me the perfect excuse, so I told him all about it. Seems Jezzer isn't the sort of bloke to be put off by a rash. Told you he was odd. Anyway, he told me it sounded like prickly heat, which his aunt used to get and he'd look it up on the internet for me. He'd told me all that stuff that I've just told you then I decided I really should tell Mandy I couldn't go. That had been the first time I called her and she'd answered then.

"I can't go, Mandy," I said. "I've got miliaria rubra."

"Crikey, Sue! That sounds bad; what is it? Are you very ill? Can I do anything? Is it contagious?" She seemed worried about me.

"Don't worry, it's not catching and it's not going to kill me. It doesn't sound so scary when it's called prickly heat."

"Prickly what?"

"Prickly heat, it's a rash and ..."

"You're right. Prickly heat doesn't sound bad," she interrupted. Sympathy didn't last long, you'll notice.

"It is. It's really itchy and …"

"Well try not to scratch it at the party."

I decided to try an approach she'd understand.

"I'll be really embarrassed with everyone looking at it and they will if I'm wearing nothing but three fig leaves."

"Wear more leaves. I'll see you at seven-thirty, just like we agreed."

Shy or bossy? I'll let you decide.

I was feeling sorry for myself when Duncan came home.

"What's up, Sis?"

I told him everything.

"You ring up Jezzer and see if there's anything he's found out that will make you feel better and I'll stick some more leaves onto your outfit."

It wasn't quite the response I'd hoped for. "You think I should go?"

"You told me that Mandy is going as a Baywatch babe but won't go without you; of course you've got to come."

I rang Jezzer. I knew he'd be nice to me.

"How are you feeling now, Sue?" he asked ever so sweetly.

"Itchy. Is there anything I can do to stop that?"

"Yes, I've been reading up on the subject since I heard you had it. Usually the problem will clear up quickly without any treatment, but calamine lotion would probably be soothing if the itching is very bad or you could ask the pharmacy for some 1% hydrocortisone cream to reduce the inflammation. The best thing you can do seems to be to stay cool and avoid sweating. You could take a cold shower and then dress in loose clothes and stay in a cool place."

"A shower sounds like a great idea. Thanks, Jez, I'll try that right away." I hung up and left him to think about me in the shower.

Whilst I was in there, I felt much better. The itching stopped and the thought of the sweat and stuff being washed away cheered me up. When I got out, I saw the rash was just as bad. I rang Mandy back and left the message saying I couldn't go – the one I told you about at the start of this story.

I rang Jezzer back. "I've still got the rash," I told him.

"It can take a few days to clear."

"I'll have to miss the party then," I pointed out.

"That would be a shame. I was really looking forward to seeing you."

I wasn't sure what to do. The idea of missing the party didn't seem such a good one by then.

"Why don't you keep as cool as you can until it's time to go and then wear cool clothing, cotton is best apparently. We could stay in the garden most of the evening and if you don't feel well, I'd be happy to bring you home at any time."

"OK then. I'll see you there."

I remembered Duncan was working on my costume. "Hold the fig leaves," I called. Before he could answer, the house phone rang.

"Hi, Mandy," he simpered. "No, don't worry, she's coming."

Anyway, to cut a long story short, I took off some of the leaves Duncan had added to my costume and turned up at the party looking like a moth-eaten bush.

"Hello, Sue. You look lovely," Jezzer said the minute we walked through the door.

"Yeah, absolutely treeeemendous," Duncan said.

"Leaf it out," Mandy giggled.

That was the last I saw of them.

"You really do look lovely," Jezzer said when they'd cleared off.

"Thanks, Jez. What have you come as, exactly?"

"An off duty air traffic controller."

"Oh, OK," was all I could say to that.

Jezzer didn't seem to have anything at all to talk about. Odd as he was quite chatty on the phone. I decided it was down to me to keep the conversation going as I'm good at that sort of thing.

"So, when you looked up about my miliaria, did you find out what caused it?" I used the posh name as I didn't fancy announcing in public that I had a rash I was worried about.

"It is just the blockage of the sweat ducts," he said. "Miliaria can develop in anyone at any age, but is most common in children and babies as their sweat glands are immature so more likely to become blocked. Another cause is people travelling to somewhere hot and sweating more than usual."

"Hmmm. I've started cycling recently and I wear lots of clothes as it's cold in the mornings, but I get sweaty on the way. Maybe that's caused it?"

"It's possible. Miliaria can occur whenever sweating is a problem. For example, if someone is ill and lies on their back for a long time they might get it on their back."

"So, can I stop it coming back?"

"You can help by trying to avoid getting hot and stay out of humid places. Even staying in a cool place for a few hours a day can help. Using an antibacterial soap or antiseptic wash might reduce the bacteria on your skin which seem to be responsible for the condition. Moisturisers containing anhydrous lanolin can help to prevent blockage of the sweat ducts. The main thing though is to keep cool. Why don't you sit out in the garden and I'll bring you a nice cold drink?"

That made sense, so I did as he suggested.

"Will I need any other treatment?" I asked when he'd given me the drink but, despite opening his mouth a few times, hadn't started talking.

"I think you'll be fine, but of course if you felt unwell you should see a doctor."

"I don't feel ill."

"That's good."

"I do feel a bit warm though."

"Perhaps you'd like to come for a drive, then? My car has air conditioning."

So that's what we did, we went for a drive. I'm not telling you what happened after that, you'll have to use your imagination. I will just say that the rash was gone a few days later and it didn't come back.

12. Making Chances

"Got a minute, Boss?"

"Not really, but come in." Mark reached for his wallet. The names for secret Santa had already been drawn, so Adam's envelope and hopeful smile meant a staff birthday or something else along those lines he was expected to contribute towards.

"It's about the Fine Chances charity. The one which helps Kristie's little girl."

"Ah." He let go of the fiver and plucked out a couple of tens. Fine Chances helped children, and the families of those children, who'd had complications at birth. Boy, had Kristie needed that help! The rat who'd got her pregnant had slunk off even before her first scan.

"I'm not collecting exactly," Adam said.

"What exactly *are* you doing?" Mark wasn't sure he wanted to know, but felt he had no choice.

"They're doing a pantomime in the sports centre, to raise funds; we want to take part. Could the company sponsor us? It would be good publicity."

"Would it?" He couldn't see it himself. Engineering companies don't need a child friendly reputation.

"Absolutely! Flexible working arrangements make you an attractive employer and allow you to give a better service and ..."

"All right. Just don't waste work time planning it." Mark's sister, who worked for the sports centre, was always wanting him to do more to show his non-existent softer side. This might get her off his back for a while. He grinned to himself; fat chance! "I want to see paperwork before I'm committed to more than this." He chucked Adam the twenty pounds.

"Thanks, Boss. You won't regret it."

So far he didn't. Kristie was a good secretary. His handwriting was awful and he was just a tiny bit difficult to get along with at times, but she always wore a smile and sometimes tempted him to return it. Although the temporary replacement was efficient, Kristie's maternity leave had been miserable for Mark.

Thankfully Arabella, Kristie's daughter, had been offered a place at Fine Chances nursery. She was soon crawling and doing most of the other stuff kids were supposed to do, and Kristie was back at work full time. Three years on, he was still grateful to Fine Chances and still trying to kid himself that his feelings for Kristie were simply those of a boss for a reliable employee.

All was fine until Mark learned what his staff had planned; a dancing on ice routine for goodness sake. What was wrong with people?

"Shall we put you down for a part?" Adam asked.

"Absolutely not! If I injured myself it'd mess up the rugby season." Wearing sequins and looking like an idiot wasn't going to impress anyone; but he kept quiet about that as the person he'd most like to impress was at her desk typing invoices.

"If you don't want to skate you could do costumes and stuff, but we'll work it out so there are easy parts, holding onto someone more skilled if necessary, so everyone who wants to join in can."

"Don't push your luck!"

He glanced at Kristie and remembered she'd been showing pictures of that kid of hers on a tricycle and how proud she'd been. Sometimes people needed help to achieve their goals and it was right that those who were able did their bit to provide it.

"I'll give you a cheque for the costumes. And I know someone at the sports centre, so I'll sort out practice sessions."

"Thanks, Boss. Very good of you."

Mark waved him away. He did call his sister to make some arrangements, but not immediately. He waited until he was home.

Adam would keep updating him on progress. "Practices are going brilliantly, Boss. There's still time to give you a part if ..." Adam trailed off, presumably because Mark's thoughts showed in his face.

He couldn't avoid attending the event. Fortunately his staff's turn earned huge cheers. From the glimpses he caught as he edged his way out, they'd not done too badly or completely embarrassed the company name. No, the announcer did that by following deserved praise for his staff by totally overdone thanks for the generosity of the sponsorship from Mark's Machines. Why all the fuss? He'd only written a cheque.

"And now it's the turn of those this evening is all about. The children will enact a charming scene from that perennial favourite, Peter Pan."

Tinkerbell's pirouettes, spirals and turns left everyone but her a little dizzy. Peter and Hook performed a thrilling high speed chase. Children who couldn't move so confidently were helped onto the ice by family and staff.

Mark's sister, in her guise of Wendy, came for them. Some were carried, others skated hand in hand with Wendy. One child followed her and they created a simple mirror dance, another took part in a pair spin. Each child was received in the centre of the rink by the dog Nana.

Mark didn't think he'd ever been so hot as he was in that dog suit, holding onto a group of excited children and ensuring their bodies were protected from the cold and their fingers clear of blades.

As they skated off to thunderous applause, Mark swung Kristie's daughter onto his shoulders. Arabella squealed in delight, unaware he was simply using her to ensure no one could whip the head from his costume and unmask him.

She bent down and whispered, "Love you, Uncle Mark."

"Love you too, sweetie," he replied before finding Kristie and handing over her daughter. Maybe one day he'd have a similar conversation with Kristie herself. Huh! Chance would be a fine thing.

Maybe it was the way the child kept his secret by calling, "Bye doggy!" or the tears of happiness in his secretary's eyes, or the cheers from the crowd as the announcer announced (as announcers do) the total reached, or a dash of festive spirit, but suddenly anything seemed possible. Mark raced to shower and join his staff for the after event / pre Christmas party.

"See, I told you there was a chance he'd join us," Adam told the others. "Can I get you a pint, Boss?"

"You can, thanks." Once they all had drinks Mark said, "To chance, what a fine thing it is." As they repeated his toast, Mark promised himself he'd try to create a few chances of his own. He edged his seat in between Adam's and Kristie's and gave her his finest smile.

13. Supergran

When I first discovered I was going to be a grandmother, I ran around telling everyone. Yes, I do mean 'ran' and 'everyone'. If I spotted a neighbour in the street, or a colleague in the corridor, I'd rush after them and tell them my news.

Of course, I did know they weren't quite as excited about the idea as I was, so I tried to ensure I only showed the same scan to the same person a maximum of three times. No, honestly, I wasn't really that bad! Not quite anyway. All my friends knew how happy I was though and there was plenty of teasing.

"All right, Grandma?" the office junior would ask. "Need any help with the stairs?"

E-mails offering Zimmer frames and stair lifts were regularly forwarded to me.

"Hiya, granny-to-be," my best friend would say when she called me. "Fancy coming out for a glass of stout and a couple of Sanatogen?"

Listening to them, you'd have thought I was seventy-five, not (just) fifty-seven. I still don't know who put me on the mailing lists, but my junk mail started to include far more adverts for mobility scooters, denture fixatives and Saga holidays than it ever used to. None of that worried me. I just knew I was going to be a fantastic grandparent.

The children (I was none to secretly hoping there would be several) wouldn't be dumped in front of the TV. Oh no! I'd take them over the park, play football with them, teach them to fly kites and ride bikes. We'd build sandcastles and go for walks. Maybe we could learn skateboarding together? That wouldn't be for a year or two. First I'd be there for my daughter, Sara, during her pregnancy and in those first few exhausting weeks after the birth. I remembered from my own experience just how tiring it can be getting used to a new baby.

To be honest it's even worse once they're toddlers. It certainly was for me. It didn't help that that's when my thyroid problem started. Absolutely wiped out I was. That's all sorted now, thanks to daily thyroxine tablets and a yearly blood test. No trouble. Where was I? Oh yes; my plans for taking care of Sara and the baby. Full of excitement and energy, I rang up and asked, almost pleaded really, what I could do to help.

"If you're really determined to help, there's plenty of decorating to do," Sara said. "You could help with painting the nursery."

I booked a week off work, packed and drove up to her place. I insisted she put her feet up as much as possible. Looking back, I see I rather took over. I did all the cooking and cleaning for Sara and Mike. They didn't seem to mind.

"Any chance of a proper roast with Yorkshire puddings, Mum? A lemon meringue pie would be good too," Mike suggested.

Whilst they were at work, I stripped the wallpaper from the room that was to be the baby's. I sanded down woodwork, filled small holes, fitted window locks and painted on the primer. When I wasn't decorating, I was out shopping for organic vegetables and baby clothes. Several evenings I took myself out, to give them both a bit of space. It was a busy time; tiring but fun too.

"You've been brilliant, Mum; a real help. Would you like to come and stay when I have the baby?"

"I'd love to, if you want me?"

"We do. We've talked about it and it'd be great to have you here," Mike said.

By the time I'd driven myself home, read my mail and watered my house plants, I was ready for bed – and it was only just after nine! It was almost as though I'd stopped taking my thyroxine medication; I felt so lethargic. Thinking it was due to nothing more than returning to an empty house and the promise of a full in-tray at work to look forward too, I headed for bed. At the top of the stairs, I felt breathless.

A good night's sleep didn't help much. I was still feeling sluggish the following morning.

"You OK, Grandma?" the junior asked. "You look a bit pale."

"Fine, thanks, Sandy. Just had a busy week, at my daughter's. I've been helping decorate the new nursery."

"I should have guessed it would be something baby related!" she said, laughing.

Over the next week, my energy levels didn't improve. Everything seemed such an effort that after work I just slumped in front of the TV. Maybe I had a bug, I thought. If so, I'd soon get better.

It wasn't a bug and I gradually got more and more tired. Walking up stairs left me out of breath and on a few occasions, I thought I might faint. Two weeks later, I realised whatever was wrong wasn't going to clear up on its own and I made an appointment to see my doctor. Actually, I only put it off that long, because I was a bit worried he might just say it was my age. For the first time, I started to feel like a grey haired walking stick wielding grandmother.

The doctor was sympathetic. "It could be a worsening of your thyroid condition, but I don't think so. We'll take a blood test to make sure and test for other things at the same time." He asked about my lifestyle, eating habits and general health. "Do you have any chest pains or palpitations?"

"No, nothing like that. I get breathless, but it's not painful. Mostly I'm just tired and don't feel like making any effort. People have said I look pale."

"You do a bit." He asked me to stick out my tongue, looked in my eyes and took my blood pressure. "I think you may be anaemic."

"I don't see how. I eat a good diet, not just some red meat, but plenty of green vegetables, fruit and all that."

He nodded. "That's good. We'll know more once you've had the blood test. The nurse can do that for you now and we should have the results in a week. I'd like you to come back and see me then."

Sure enough, the nurse took a few samples of blood. It didn't hurt, but I don't like to watch, so I turned my head and distracted myself by telling her about my expected grandchild.

A week later, I was back at the doctor's.

"The good news is that I know what's wrong and it's easily treatable," he said.

"That's good. Do I take it there's some bad news?"

"Some. Perhaps I should explain your condition?"

"Please."

"As I thought, you do have pernicious anaemia. All the other tests were fine. Your thyroid function is being well controlled with the medication, and everything else we tested for was negative."

"Good, so do I have to live on spinach and liver?"

He smiled. "No. Your diet isn't the problem. You're eating enough B12, but your body isn't making use of it."

"B12? I thought anaemia was lack of iron?"

"Not precisely, although that can cause anaemia. Anaemia is either a lack of red blood cells or less haemoglobin than normal in those blood cells. Both are needed to carry oxygen around your body in the bloodstream."

I knew I needed oxygen in my blood, but wasn't sure why I didn't have enough. "So where does the B12 come in?"

"Along with iron and other vitamins, it's needed to keep your bone marrow healthy. Bone marrow is where the red blood cells are made."

"Right. So, I just need to get some B12 tablets and I'll be OK?"

He shook his head. "Not tablets, injections."

"I'd rather have tablets doctor. I'm used to taking them already; one more wouldn't make much difference."

"Tablets won't help."

"Oh. That's right, you said I was eating enough B12 anyway. If there's enough of it, what's going wrong?"

"Antibodies are being formed against your intrinsic factor, this stops it binding with the B12 and so the vitamin cannot be absorbed by your body. It's due to an autoimmune disease."

"Can you explain the science bit again – slowly?"

"Sorry, yes. Normally when you eat foods containing B12, the vitamin combines in the stomach with a protein called intrinsic factor. That's made by your own body in your stomach and then absorbed lower down in your gut. In your case, the antibodies that usually attack bacteria and viruses are attacking either the intrinsic factor or the cells that make it."

That was starting to sound familiar. "Isn't it something like that which is causing my thyroid problem? Is this connected?"

"That's right. Pernicious anaemia is more common in those who already have another autoimmune disease, such as the one resulting in your underactive thyroid."

I thought I understood, but it was a bit complicated. "So, the B12 is there, but because of this disease, it isn't being absorbed in my gut. That means my bone marrow isn't making enough red blood cells and that makes me anaemic.?"

"Exactly."

"So, the B12 injections mean I get the stuff direct, without having to absorb it?"

"Right again."

"Will I need them every day?" I didn't fancy that at all. One of the girls at work is diabetic and has to inject herself. She says it's OK once you're used to it, but I'd rather not have to do it.

"No. You'll need quite a few to start with. Six in fact and they'll be just a couple of days apart. Once you've built up a good supply of B12, it will be stored in your liver and you will only need to have a top up every three months."

"Oh, that's not so bad. Is that it?"

"That will fix the anaemia and you'll soon be back to your old self, but …"

"Here, less of the old. D'you know, I was wondering if this was all 'just my age'?"

"It does usually start over the age of fifty, but I agree you're not old and soon you won't feel it either."

"Thanks. You said, 'but'."

"Yes, there is some bad news. Having pernicious anaemia does make you more likely to develop stomach cancer. Because of that, it's important you don't ignore regular stomach pains or persistent indigestion."

"OK, I'll make an appointment if anything seems wrong. How likely is the cancer?"

"There is about a four in a hundred chance of you developing it."

I nodded whilst I took that in. My thoughts went to my daughter and the baby. "Is this hereditary? The anaemia, I mean."

"It does tend to run in families, but that doesn't mean your family are certain to develop it. Women are most often affected and as I said, those who already have an autoimmune disease."

Of course, I got the injections. I didn't fancy the idea, but as it turned out, they weren't really much different than the blood tests. Almost immediately, I started feeling better, it was amazing. I had another test to ensure everything was OK. It was. I'll now need an annual blood test to keep an eye on things. That shouldn't be a problem though, I can have it done at the same time as my thyroid test and one of the top ups for B12. Anyway, I can't stop to chat.

Sara's baby is due tomorrow and I've got a final bit of packing to do. Mike asked me to make a soufflé, so I'll need my proper dish to cook it in. I need to find my rechargeable screwdriver to fix up the stair gate I've bought. My gardening things are already packed as I've offered to sort out the flower beds and make sure all the plants in crawling range are child friendly. Well, I'm not old or ill and I don't want to sit around in front of the TV the whole time I'm there!

14. Beach Body

Are you beach body ready?

It's easy to tell if your body is 'beach ready'. First you need to dress (or undress) it in whatever you'd like to wear on the beach. Next you need to take it to the beach and wait three minutes. If it doesn't run away really fast, it was ready.

If it does run away, it was probably just hot. Buy it an ice cream and try again later.

15. Loneliness

Loneliness is not just being on your own. It isn't being the only person who lives in your house. It's not taking a long country walk and meeting no one. That's being alone, in simple solitude. Loneliness is something different, something that lurks deep inside you, nibbling at your soul. It lessens and reduces you, until you become the nothing that your lonely heart believes you to be.

Walking down the street you do not hold your head high looking out for friends. You keep it down; you mustn't make eye contact with a stranger. They might see your despair, feel your sorrow. You don't need their pity.

Loneliness is hearing your name called and knowing it's not you who is sought. Another girl with the same first name has an acquaintance, a friend, perhaps a lover who wishes to attract her attention. To call her close, to talk, to be with her. Don't look round, no one wants you.

Loneliness is hearing the postman whistle as he pushes mail through your door. No need to hurry, you can pay that bill later. The letter from your MP claims he wants to know what you think. He doesn't – he just wants your vote. Did you look, hoping for a letter from a friend? Who would write that then?

Loneliness is a chicken quarter and individual fruit sponge for Christmas lunch. A card that says 'best wishes to all at No.53 from Viv and Chris at No.57' and you don't know which is the husband and which the wife. A miniature bottle of wine as a treat. A pack of mince pies in case people call, which you give to the birds in January.

You are lonely, and in that at least you are not alone. The widower who brings the Betterware catalogue, he's just as lonely as you. Viv who wrote the Christmas card is lonely too, she lost the baby she was carrying. Her husband is too full of grief to comfort her. The girl you see walking to the bus stop each morning misses her fiancé who has sailed with his ship, not due back before July. The new dispenser in the chemist shop has just moved here, he doesn't know anyone.

The friend you hoped would write to you, does she look hopefully through her mail hoping to hear from you? The neighbours who didn't eat your mince pies, did you invite them? Those people who walk past without greeting you, have you ever smiled and said, 'good morning' to them?

Lift up your head and smile. Make a phone call. Pick up a pen and write. Stop for a moment and talk. The world is full of lonely people. You don't have to be one of them.

16. When The Chips Are Down

My husband, John, had been working away for months. I was pleased his new job meant he was based at home, even though it often involved long hours. He called me one afternoon, just as I was preparing to leave my office. I nearly didn't answer the phone, I'd planned to get away on time, race home and prepare for a relaxing evening together.

"Sorry, Jane love. Something's come up."

"You mean you'll be late home again. Should I plan to cook dinner a bit later?"

"Forget it altogether more like, I won't be finished to gone nine at the earliest."

I made it clear I wasn't happy.

"You could come in and sit with me. At least we could talk a bit and then I'll get us a takeaway on the way home."

It was almost ten by the time we were on our way home. I hadn't eaten since midday, so I was really hungry.

"What do you fancy to eat?" John asked.

"Whatever's quickest, preferably something I can eat straight away."

As I spoke, we passed a chicken and chip place.

"That do?"

"Right now, I'd eat a scabby dog if it was well cooked."

He took that as a yes and found a parking space.

"Two large chicken and chips please," John said.

"We're just packing up, you can have some ribs as well if you like? Save us chucking them out," the lady behind the counter offered. She packaged up our food quickly. We were given so many chips she couldn't close the boxes properly. Another box was filled with ribs and BBQ sauce.

We drove down to the seafront and ate the lot.

As we got into bed, I mentioned that I'd eaten too much.

"Yeah, me too. Still, just once won't do us any harm."

Later in the night, my stomach started to hurt. I felt sick and before long, I made a dash for the bathroom and threw up. I still had a pain in the morning, but as John was fine, I knew food poisoning was unlikely. I thought I'd just eaten too much greasy food too quickly, then not digested it before going to bed. It would be enough to make anyone ill. Well, anyone except John, but then he hasn't had any medical problems since he had measles aged six.

I went to work and apart from not wanting to eat, I started to feel better. By the time I was home again, I had no more than a bruised feeling on my right side, just below my ribs. I thought that was because I'd been sick. John persuaded me to eat something that evening. I soon started feeling unwell again. The pain was severe, not in my belly, but just below my ribs. I felt hot and vomited again. I felt dreadfully ill and just wanted to sleep. John tried to persuade me to get into bed. I tried to tell him why I couldn't, but instead I was sick again – on him. Once I'd stopped, he carried me to bed. In the morning, I felt sick again, I made another dash for the bathroom, but was too weak to get there. By that time, I was bringing up nothing but a bitter yellow liquid.

I lay on the top of the stairs, whimpering with pain. John wrapped a quilt round me and called the NHS helpline and was advised to take me to the local hospital. Perhaps because he's never needed one, John hates hospitals, but he didn't hesitate. He somehow got me into the car and then into the hospital. I don't remember much about that trip. John tells me the doctor ruled out appendicitis and an ectopic pregnancy. He said I was weak because of dehydration and gave me an injection to stop me being sick. I was crying with the pain.

John took me home after I was advised to contact my GP on Monday if I was no better. The injection stopped me being sick and after I'd drunk some tea I felt slightly better. I didn't eat anything for fear of being sick. I was still in pain and feeling generally unwell.

On Monday, I rang my doctor and was told to come in at the end of surgery. My GP examined me and said she thought I might have an infection in my gall bladder.

"You'll need to have an ultrasound scan to be sure, but in the meantime don't eat anything with any fat in it."

"Was it the chips that caused this then?"

"They won't have helped, but you've most likely had a problem for some time without realising it. With some people, there are stones that cause pain. You may have stones, or perhaps have just developed an infection. The scan will show us."

"Then what will happen?"

"It depends on the scan, but the most likely outcome is that your gall bladder will be removed."

"Don't I need it?" I asked. "Isn't that where bile is stored?" I could remember from biology lessons at school, that bile was needed to digest food.

"It is, but without it, bile will still be produced. It will drain constantly into the gut, rather than there being a surge when you eat. Large fatty meals might be a problem, but if you eat healthily you'll be fine."

I was given some tablets to take if I felt sick again.

I had more questions, but thought I should wait until the diagnosis was confirmed, so I didn't start fretting over things which might never happen. I tried really hard to avoid all fat in my diet. I got quite a shock when I read the details on the backs of ready meals; I couldn't eat any of them. Grilling a chicken breast or piece of fish without adding fat was easy enough. Eating it with nothing but steamed veg was a bit dull, but OK and it was worth it. After a few days, the pain was completely gone.

I didn't have long to wait for my scan. It was the same as they do for pregnant women. When I got to hospital, I was introduced to a trainee technician. I was asked if I would mind him examining me. I was assured that the scan would be repeated by an experienced member of staff. I agreed. It would help the chap learn and I knew I'd be getting a thorough check. Jelly was spread on my stomach and then the scanner moved across my belly. It didn't hurt, even when it was pressed on the area over my gallbladder.

"Found it," the trainee said.

He pointed out something on the screen to his colleague.

"What is it? Have I got gallstones?" I asked.

"Take a look," the screen was turned round. On it was some squidgy grey stuff which was the scan of my insides. There was a clearly defined egg shaped thing in the centre.

"There's your stone."

"Just one?" I couldn't believe one tiny stone had caused so much pain. I felt a bit of a fraud as I remembered my mum had suffered with gallstones. She'd had recurring pains for some time and when they removed her gallbladder there were nearly twenty stones.

"How much is that magnified?" I asked.

"It isn't." I was told. "If there's just one then they often are big, yours is pretty impressive."

"That must be painful," the trainee said.

"It was a few weeks ago, it's OK now."

"The gallbladder is still badly inflamed. You'll probably need to have it removed, but that's best done when the inflammation is reduced."

"Probably? Isn't that what normally happens then?"

"If there is pain or infection then yes, but many people who have gall stones will experience very little pain. In that case, there's no need for surgery. I don't make that decision though. That's for the surgeon and you to work out."

Although I didn't fancy an operation, I was relieved that I knew what was wrong and that it was treatable.

Not long after the scan, I was invited to have a consultation with a surgeon. He confirmed that I had a single large gallstone.

"What makes the stones then?"

"Gallstones are just bile that has hardened, often there are solidified lumps of cholesterol too."

"Could I have avoided having this?"

"No. Being obese increases your risk slightly and a vegetarian diet might reduce it, but one in three women and one in six men will get them. Most won't experience pain or require treatment. Only about a third of those with stones will ever be aware of them. In your case, the stone is clearly causing a great deal of discomfort and has lead to infection. That's likely to recur. I would suggest that the best treatment is to remove both the stone and the gallbladder."

I nodded my agreement. I never wanted to go through that pain again.

"You'll have a laparoscopic cholecystectomy. That just means that I will use a telescope device to see what I'm doing. It's what's known as keyhole surgery. The scarring won't be bad and you'll recover quickly."

Three months after I'd first had the pain, I went in for the operation. John still hated hospitals, but he took me in and sat with me for as long as he was allowed. I knew he wasn't comfortable and teased him about it.

"Don't worry, they won't take you by mistake."

"I wish they didn't have to take you either," he said. "but if it will stop you throwing up on me, I suppose it's worth it."

Afterwards I was in quite a lot of pain, but not as bad as when I'd had the infection. John was there when I was wheeled back to the ward. He held my hand as he waited for me to come round properly.

Instead of stitches, I had big metal staples. They looked awful. I was told they were easier to remove than traditional stitches. I was allowed home that evening. Getting in and out of bed was painful and I needed help the first few days. Each day I improved, by the time I needed to have the staples removed, I was able to walk to the surgery. I returned to work twelve days after the operation.

Two years on the scars are hardly noticeable and there's no discomfort at all. I've heard some people have to be careful not to eat much fatty food, but luckily for me I don't have any digestive problems whatever I eat.

My husband still sometimes works long hours. I still occasionally sit with him, but for some reason he hasn't bought me chips on the way home since.

17. You Are What You Eat

McDonalds and Pizzas, Kentucky and chips,
Make my mouth water, as they cross my lips.

Fresh fruit and vegetables? They're just not cool,
Healthy eating's not really done at my school.

Crisps and chocolate, great mouthfuls of Coke,
Wholegrain and salads? They'd just make me choke.

I'm fat and I'm spotty, I'm not very fit,
You others go play, I'll rest for a bit.

I'm badly behaved, my school work is poor.
To cheer myself up, I open the fridge door.

I'll never be healthy, or live to grow old,
You are what you eat, or so we are told.

Are you worried this sounds slightly like you?
If you want to change – then here's what to do.

Patsy Collins

Take a long walk, or get on your bike,
Swim or play football, whatever you like.

Then you'll be hungry and ready for dinner.
The right sort of food, will help you get thinner.

Fruits and veggies, grains, rice, seeds and salad too.
These are the foods that are good for you.

Perhaps some chicken, eggs or nice piece of fish.
Add plenty of veggies to fill up your dish.

With fresh fruits or yoghurt for your dessert,
These dietary changes really won't hurt.

An orange a day helps the body fight infection.
It's got vitamin C and is great for the complexion.

Ask for crisp carrot sticks in your lunch box,
Is your mum ready, for these little shocks?

You'll look much better, and feel just great,
If you're sensible about what goes on your plate.

18. How Long?

Dave Farrow was dying.

Doctors had always dismissed his symptoms but this new chap took him seriously.

The private consultant examined, queried and actually listened. Gravely he said, "I must inform you your life-span is limited, Mr Farrow."

Dave clutched his chest. The palpitations were back. His heart was still beating though. "Please don't tell me how long I have left." He'd lived for years in terror of the unknown disease which gnawed away at his health and happiness. Now his fears were proven justified he could at last face them.

"As you wish. You'll feel quite well for a time. I suggest you make the most of that."

"I shall, doctor. Thank you."

Dave's lethargy retreated. His pains and swollen glands disappeared. He no longer heard the ringing in his ears. The useless pills and tablets were thrown away. Medical text books abandoned in favour of delicious recipes, concert programmes, and maps.

The world, once a source of danger and contamination was now another place. A great big, fascinating planet and his to explore. Dave no longer cut himself off from his fellow man. He made friends and let them get close without concern of infection. He left his home without worrying where the nearest hospital might be. He tried new foods without fearing intestinal reactions. Instead of recording body temperature, bowel movements, and blood pressure in his diary he noted things he'd enjoyed or which he hoped to experience.

For almost a year he was happy. As his annual check-up neared he regretted the wasted years. No! He wouldn't allow negativity to ruin whatever remained of his life. Life wasn't over yet.

Bravely he asked, "Doctor, how much longer?"

"Approximately forty-seven years, Mr Farrow. Use them well."

Dave stared. "I'll be in my nineties by then."

"Yes. That's the expected lifespan for a healthy man which is, and always has been, what you are."

Dave shook his head. Slowly he raised himself from the chair. "I'll be in touch, doctor."

"But you don't need me, Mr Farrow. Really you don't."

"I'm going to send you a postcard every year so you can see if you're right."

"Where are you going?"

"I don't know, but I'll enjoy it." Dave turned and walked towards the horizon.

19. The Best Is Yet To Come

I can do this. Five more steps and I'll have accomplished my goal of walking on top of the mountain. I grip my hiking poles tightly and move my right leg forward. Nearly there. It's been a long and difficult journey, but I *will* complete it.

"You can do this, Merryn," echoes in my mind. So many people have told me that's true and helped make it possible in so many different ways. Today is for them, but for myself too. And for Neil.

I turn to the man by my side. "Nearly there, Neil. You can do this."

"We can, Merryn," he assures me.

It started about a year ago, I suppose. Five of us who were going through chemotherapy formed a kind of club. Mostly we chatted online, but met in person too when our immune systems allowed. We all had support from friends or family and brilliant medical staff, but it was good to talk with people who were going through it. Who really understood. People with whom we were normal, not the exception. Who could tell us the weird tacky sensation when we touched our head and face, or the way we always seemed to have grit in our eye weren't further worrying symptoms, just the result of hair loss. The group became an even better source of encouragement when the first two had come through chemo. Who'd left the side effects, and the reason we endured them, behind. For whom the worst was over and the best was yet to come.

Maybe it will seem odd, but we rarely mentioned cancer. We had the odd moan about treatments, sometimes discussed what kind friends and family were doing to support us, or shared how we were feeling. Most often though we talked about life before and after. Before was our starting point, after our destination. Cancer was just the journey between. We didn't believe that all the time, but it helped to try to think of it that way.

We often talked about amazing bucket list trips and journeys of a lifetime. Those we'd made already, those we had planned, and those which seemed impossible dreams. Louise showed us selfies of her in small bikinis and the company of handsome men, and looked forward to taking more such photos. Tom told us about wonderful food he'd eaten and fabulous souvenirs he'd brought back and where he hoped to find such temptations in future. Neil's photos were of his campervan parked by gorgeous deserted beaches.

"I'd be happy to take everyone out somewhere," he offered.

"Even happier if it was just one of us," Tash muttered. She'd hinted more than once that Neil is 'fond of you' as she puts it. I was sure she'd misinterpreted his kindness in cheering me up when I felt ugly and of no use to anyone. Neil is kind. Tash is no fool, but she's as optimistic as she is romantic.

"I was thinking of a day trip," Neil said.

"As long as it's somewhere I can treat us to a nice meal, rather than share a can of beans, I'm in," Tom said.

After we'd made a pact to do that, I told them about my visit to the pyramids. "It's incredible that you can still touch all that history."

"Literally touch?" Neil asked.

"Yes. In theory you could climb up to the top."

"Not me!" he hastily declared.

"Nor me," I admitted. "In pictures it looks like they're stepped all the way up. Actually, they really are, but those stone blocks are way bigger than I'd realised. Without the proof before me I'd have said it would be impossible for people to put even one on top of another."

Life's like that I've discovered recently. A series of steps, some of which look easy, some which seem impossible. Either way, and regardless of whether or not those initial impressions are deceptive, our only real choice is to keep climbing.

"Weren't they all on drugs when they built them?" Louise asked.

"Get me those drugs!" Tash said, making us laugh. She's the oldest of us and says she was so square she really can remember the sixties. "I'm making up for it now though." She doesn't have stronger painkillers than she actually needs, but enjoys playing the spaced out hippy to raise people's spirits. Her bright, flower power clothing makes me smile.

"Bet with the right meds I could climb Machu Picchu," Tash declared.

Tom briefly rested his hand on her shoulder. "Of course you could."

Tash pulled out her phone and tapped away. "Blow that! It says here there's a four day hike. I don't mind climbing a mountain, but I'm not walking there first!"

"There's the difference between us," said Neil who is almost two feet taller and four decades younger than Tash, "I'm happy to walk as far as you like, as long as there aren't any heights involved." He was brave about every part of his treatment from surgery to hair loss, except it being on the seventh floor.

"It's the nights between which would worry me," Tom said. "I went glamping once and let me tell you, nothing to do with inflatable beds and no room service is glam."

"Let's face it," Louise said. "None of us has ever climbed a mountain and never will."

"We'll have none of that talk, young lady!" Tash reprimanded her. She's not into negativity is Tash, and she doesn't let us get away with it either.

"Sorry. I didn't mean we couldn't, just that we probably won't."

"Definitely won't," said Neil. "But not because I can't."

"I used to," I said. "Well, really big hills mostly, but I did a fair bit of climbing." I passed Tash my phone to show a photo of me, tired but happy, posing on High Willhays Tor. I didn't say I still could, and didn't expect the others to say it either. You need a pair of hiking boots to do that kind of thing, and more than one foot to put in them.

I described other trips. A safari. A couple of wonderful cruises. They were things I could still do, but I couldn't stop my thoughts and words returning to the mountains. My new friends were impressed, but they were an easy crowd. Some of those who now belong to the past weren't. Ben Nevis might be the UK's highest mountain and a huge challenge to many, but those who consider themselves true adventurers are sniffy about anywhere with sign posts and a footpath to get you started. I confess I was a little myself that way at one time, but things change. I'd changed.

My self-confidence had gone. That wasn't all down to cancer, not directly. The man I thought loved me not only thought mountains with footpaths weren't worth climbing, he also thought he was doing me a massive favour by not dumping me the minute he learned I needed an amputation. I overheard him talking about his noble sacrifice to a friend and put an end to it.

When Neil heard why I was single he didn't call my ex selfish and shallow as Tom and Louise did, nor use any of Tash's newly mastered colourful words. He called him an idiot and asked me out. I called myself an idiot for the horribly awkward way in which I turned him down.

"I'm sorry, Merryn," he said, though I wasn't sure what he was apologising for.

"I'm sorry too." That wasn't an apology, but an expression of regret.

Some weeks later I steered the conversation back to my travels.

"Which was the best trip?" Louise asked.

"The best is yet to come." It's our unofficial motto – not that we have an official one.

"Another cruise?" Tom guessed. That would be his own preference I'm sure.

"No, another mountain."

They look surprised and a little worried.

"And I want you all to come with me."

Three of them looked less worried, Neil more so.

"I know it will take a while before I can do it, but I'm determined. Tash, it's not Machu Picchu, but neither is there a four day hike to the base. Tom, there's a cafe and gift shop and although an overnight stay won't be needed there are plenty of nice hotels nearby if you want to stay on. Louise – handsome mountain rescue guys! Neil, if you say yes, so will I."

"Merryn, how can I climb a mountain when I couldn't do anything like that before?" he asked.

"You're a different person now. Stronger, more determined," I told him.

"What is it you'll say yes to?" Tash asked me.

"She means that if we say we'll climb a mountain she will too," Louise said.

"Yes, I do – but not just that."

"You spoke as though this isn't hypothetical," Tom said. "You have a real mountain in mind?"

"I do."

"One we can all climb?" Neil asked.

"Not exactly… We can all go up and walk half a dozen steps. The others can walk further if they like, but I don't want to wait long enough to be able to do that. You and I can just take a few steps, not too near the edge. That will be hard for both of us, but we can do it together."

"When do we go?" Neil asked.

On the first date we were all free, the five of us drove to Snowdon in Neil's campervan. We used my blue badge to park very near the platform for the steam train which would take us right up to the summit. Tom, Louise and Tash headed for the gift shop. Because my prosthetic was still uncomfortable to wear for long periods I'd removed it for the journey. Now I had to strap it back on. Neil stood chatting to me as I fitted it. That helped provide some privacy from other car park users, but his random disjointed sentences also revealed his nerves.

"I want to walk by myself at the top, but can I lean on you to get to the train?" I asked him.

"Of course."

By the time we reached the steam train the others had joined us. Neil sat by my side and I squeezed his hand.

"You can do this," I told him.

"We can."

And we do. For an hour the little train clatters its way up the mountainside – and four of us chatter as we admire the views and distract Neil's attention from the fact that more and more of what we can see is below us.

At the summit Neil helps me from the train and then steps aside. I grip my walking poles tightly, probably looking as though I negotiated the path rather than rode up. I take a step with my left leg, then swing my right forward.

I turn to the man by my side. "Nearly there, Neil. You can do this."

Another step. Halfway. Another step. Another. Another. I've done it; I've walked half a dozen steps on top of the mountain.

I'm not alone. "You've done it, Neil." I'm proud of him. He didn't let go of my hand the whole way up, but once out of the train he released it. He's let me walk up here unaided, because he knows it's was what I needed to do, even though it meant he too has walked, has faced his fear of heights, without help.

"I said yes and now, I hope, you will," he says.

He looks more nervous now, which stops me blurting out 'of course'. Just as well as he's not asking the question I'd expected – will I go out with him. He's not speaking at all, but holding out a small box.

I take it, flip it open and see the diamond sparkle.

Without the poles for support, my one and a half legs give way. Neil catches me and holds me tight. When the others return from their longer mountain-top walk my fiancé is still holding me.

Now we've proved we can do it alone, we walk to meet them – together.

20. The Kindness Of Sisters

"I'm thinking of applying for a job," I told my sister.

"Are you sure that's a good idea, Annette?" Caitlyn asked, her face full of concern. "People can be unkind." She glanced at my ample figure.

I knew she was right, but wasn't sure everyone was as cruel as she claimed. Despite her urging me to stay home and avoid unpleasantness, I'd ventured out occasionally recently and it wasn't so bad. I didn't kid myself I'd attracted admiring glances everywhere I went, but without Caitlyn there to draw my attention to it, I didn't notice people laughing or staring.

"You don't need to work, I'll look after you," Caitlyn said, laying a slender fingered hand on my meaty arm.

The two of us lived in the house we inherited after our parents' accident. By looking after me she meant paying the bills, buying groceries and being my only friend. In return I cleaned, did her laundry, kept the garden tidy and made sure no dark roots ever showed at the base of her honey blonde hair. That was only fair when the money she'd have spent in a salon was used to ensure I could always find a tasty treat whenever I opened the fridge.

I rarely had to cook for Caitlyn as boyfriends were always taking her to fancy restaurants. We had a pact to stay out the way if either of us brought someone home.

Maybe if I ever meet someone who wants to come back she'll realise keeping out of sight doesn't mean not hearing everything which goes on. It wasn't something I felt I could mention.

"You've done so much," I told her. She has, but somehow her attempts to protect me haven't been wholly positive. I've lost confidence and gained weight. I've even stopped suggesting we sell our large home and each buy somewhere more modest. As Caitlyn said, I wouldn't be any happier living alone.

"You're my little sister – it's my job to help you. If getting a job is what you want, I'll help with that. It might be a good idea to lose a few pound first," Caitlyn said. "Boost your confidence."

"Maybe," I agreed.

"Have you thought what kind of job you'd do?"

"I trained to be a nanny," I reminded her.

"You didn't finish though, didn't take the final exam."

"I'd been doing well …" I wanted to explain, again, it didn't work like that. We were assessed throughout the course and I'd done enough to qualify before our parents died. I couldn't get the words out.

"I know, I know," Caitlyn soothed.

"I'm sure I'll find something," I said.

"Of course you will, Annette," she said kindly.

The following day she ordered in pizza and ice cream, in case I was tired after job hunting.

"Didn't we decide I should lose weight first?" I asked.

"Oh! Yes. Sorry, Annette I didn't think."

"Never mind. You've ordered it now. One day won't make much difference, will it?"

When the doorbell sounded she asked me to clear the coffee table, so we could eat as we watched TV. It wouldn't have occurred to me the delivery guy was treated to a view of my jiggly bum if Caitlyn hadn't said, "How rude was that?" as she put the pizzas on the table now cleared of her clutter.

"What?" I asked. All I'd heard was him confirming he'd given her everything she'd ordered.

"The way he said 'extra large' while looking right at you!"

I shrugged. "Like you said, people can be unkind."

Caitlyn wasn't unkind. She gave me a huge box of the most wonderful chocolates for my birthday a few days later. "I got them before you decided to diet," she explained. "Besides, I don't think you should give up everything nice. Having a few treats might help you stick to it."

That sounded plausible. As did her explanation that cheesy pasta with garlic bread was the only thing she knew how to make when she decided to cook as a thank you for all I do for her.

Caitlyn bought me energy drinks to help me exercise, not realising the energy was all empty, sugary calories, and that she'd talked me out of jogging and aerobics because someone as unfit as me might get an injury. She kept offering me snacks as she'd read that grazing on small meals burned more fat than eating the few large meals which she couldn't have noticed I was still consuming at the mealtimes we shared more and more frequently. She took over the gardening so she could work on her tan, and save me from the embarrassment of being seen getting hot and sweaty in shorts and a tee-shirt, forgetting that was one of the few energetic activities I didn't mind.

"I'm so sorry, I'm not helping much, am I?" she said.

"It doesn't matter, Caitlyn," I assured her. "As soon as you promised you'd help me find a job I knew that weirdly all your kindness and support would backfire and you'd somehow make me so late for the interview I missed it completely. Or write a hilariously terrible joke reference to make me laugh and accidentally send it. Or put the offer of employment letter in a safe place and forget about it meaning I didn't see it and never accepted."

"What are you saying?"

"That I let you think I was following your advice to lose weight first and let you 'help' me with that, while in fact my real goal was to get a job. But don't worry, you really did help with that by reminding me of my qualification and how living alone probably wouldn't suit me."

"I don't understand."

"I applied to be a nanny. The job is live-in – and I start next week."

I offered to show her how the washing machine and vacuum worked before I left. Well, she's my big sister, it's my job to help her, and it was the kind thing to do.

21. A Game Of Conkers

"I've got something to show you," Steff said, pulling things from her tote bag.

"You're challenging me to a game of conkers?" Ashley asked.

"What? Oh, no. I meant these." She handed her friend the leaflets and returned the conkers and other debris to her bag.

Steff watched her friend look through the properties she and her boyfriend were considering buying. Ashley frowned.

"I know they're not as pretty as my cottage, but we don't want to over-reach ourselves."

"That's sensible, but they're all miles away from the school," Ashley said.

"I have long holidays and finish work early in the afternoons, so the drive won't really be a problem for me."

"So says Tyler!"

He had said it, but that didn't make it any less true. Steff was a primary school teacher. Although, as with other teachers, she often worked outside of term time and school hours, she still finished at three most days. She hadn't had to commute during August when their picturesque seaside village had been full of holidaymakers. Now term had started she enjoyed the short drive through the tree-lined lanes. If she moved away she'd miss seeing them colour in autumn, stark over winter and the first flush of green in spring.

"He's a bully, Steff, you'd be better off without him."

"He's not a bully, he's …"

Steff's phone rang. "Sorry," she said and answered it. She'd previously explained she might need to, as her sister was expecting her second baby.

"Sorry," Ashley said again. "I have to go."

"Give her my best and let me know when I can see the little one."

"I will, but I'll be watching to make sure you don't pinch it!"

Steff laughed. Her love of children was no secret and she knew her friend was joking. Thirty year old Steff wasn't ready for motherhood, wasn't even sure she ever would be. Ashley knew that, but many others assumed that's what she wanted. Tyler did, and she was sure that maternity leave had often been at the back of people's minds during job interviews.

As Steff drove home she thought about what she'd have said had Ashley's sister not called. Tyler wasn't a bully – he wasn't aggressive, didn't make jokes at her expense or criticise her in front of others. He was just more decisive than her. She'd been content in her cute mid terrace cottage, so not given any thought to where else she might want to live.

Tyler knew. He wanted somewhere with more than one bedroom, a bathroom large enough for an actual bath, a garage or driveway so he didn't have to park in the road, a living room with a straight wall to hang a flat screen TV and enough space to invite his mates round to watch the match. As he'd pointed out, somewhere like that in the pretty village where she currently lived was well beyond their means. They'd have to live in one of the nearby towns. As Steff would have a fairly long drive whichever they chose, it made sense to live near where he worked. And where his mates and family lived. Anyway, she could always switch to a different school, couldn't she?

"What you got there?" Tyler asked when he came in.

"Conkers. I'm teaching the children about games. I was going to collect enough for the whole class, but decided it would be more fun for them to collect their own. I'm going to ask the head if I can take them on a field trip."

"Don't bother," Tyler said.

"Why not?"

"You won't be able to let the kids play conkers. It's been banned due to all this health and safety woke rubbish."

Steff didn't bother telling him wokeness and health and safety were very different things and neither were rubbish. Tyler got a bee in his bonnet when he thought 'they' were telling him what to do and think.

"Playing conkers hasn't been banned." She'd heard some schools had taken that step, but not hers.

Tyler must have realised her source of information might be at least equal to his own because he didn't argue, just warned her, "Don't blame me when you get sued 'cause they break their fingers and get stuff in their eyes."

"I won't, don't worry." That wasn't the kind of game she had in mind for her class.

Steff's Friday field trip was a great success. As well as gathering plenty of conkers she was able to show them how to identify different types of tree, and through finding seedlings and fallen coloured leaves, introduce them to the life cycle of plants.

Back in the classroom she set the children the task of using their conkers in different games. "You can add things to the conkers, or decorate them however you like. You might like to include them in games you already play, or ask your family for ideas, or even make up your own. On Monday we'll all try playing the different games. There will be a gold star for anyone who makes a game which other people enjoy playing."

Steff's idea was to encourage them to use their imaginations and to think of others. She hadn't ruled out the traditional game, but was hopeful there would be alternatives.

She wasn't disappointed. Three girls who seemed almost inseparable must have spent the entire weekend painting scores of conkers. Steff couldn't imagine how they'd managed to get anything to stick to the shiny surface, but they had. Each had a different, brightly coloured, pattern. Some were spotted or striped, others marbled, or covered with tiny rainbows, flowers or love hearts.

"They're beautiful!" Steff declared with complete honesty.

"Please, can I have one?" asked another girl in the class.

"You have to win them," explained Ava, one of their creators. "Miss, can I draw on the floor with chalk?"

"Let's go outside for this, shall we?" Steff suggested.

Outside Ava drew a large circle on the playground and placed some of the decorated conkers inside. She gave the girl who'd requested one a handful of different conkers. Those two were painted, but each in a single colour.

"You have to throw them, and if you knock one of ours out then you win it."

The game, an adaptation of marbles, was such a success that Steff had to draw it to a close long before everyone had tried as many times as they'd have liked. "Maybe you can play in break time," she said as she handed out three gold stars. "Has anyone else got a game which is best played outside?"

"We have, Miss!"

Twins Kayla and Kim produced conkers on string. They all had smiley faces put on with glue and glitter. They demonstrated their game which was played just like the traditional version, except that before using their conker to whack their opponent's, they told a joke. The jokes were awful, but Steff was delighted. Not only had they lessened the aggressive nature of the usual game, they'd made it more entertaining for onlookers.

Jackson challenged the winner. His jokes were so good that Steff awarded him his own gold star when she gave Kayla and Kim theirs.

Jackson's own game involved hiding a conker under one of three cups, then moving them around and inviting people to guess its location. Sleight of hand wasn't one of his skills, but as everyone enjoyed listening to his 'patter' as he tried to distract them, and was happy not to be deceived, he earned another gold star.

One boy brought in a solitaire board, where the usual counters had been replaced by conkers. Another child had done the same thing with a drafts board. Neither had taken much effort, but the games worked and class members were happy to try them out, so they'd done what was required. Others had gone to more trouble. There were decorated cups for a complicated catching game which nobody, even the creator, quite understood, but everyone seemed to enjoy.

Jasmin had brought in a whole box of toys and figures, half of which were dressed in blue and half in red. They were football teams and the conker was the ball. She proceeded to give everyone their own player and instruct them in the rules of the game. Thanks to her, Steff finally understood the offside rule and why penalties were so important.

By the time reds had won seven goals to six, with wheelchair bound Cash having scored an ecstatic hat trick, Steff thought Jasmin deserved a whole sheet of gold stars.

"It sounded as though your class were having fun," the head said at break time.

"So much fun, and me too."

"You achieved your aim then?"

"Yes, I'm sure I did. Most had put a lot of thought into their games and a great deal of time creating them. Others not quite so much."

"You'd expect that."

"Absolutely. What I hadn't expected was their reactions when playing. To 'win' at this task didn't involve beating anyone else, but in entertaining them. The two with drafts and solitaire were good at showing the others how to play. They suggested moves and tried to explain why those might be good choices, but didn't take over. Jackson's game wasn't very good, but he's such a nice boy that everyone laughed with him and pretended to be surprised they'd won – that could so easily have gone differently. They're such great kids."

"They are and a lot of that is down to you. It's important for teachers to put knowledge and skills into their pupils and most of those I've come across do that pretty well, you included. Where you're exceptional is in getting the best out of them. Because you believe in their good points, you let those aspects shine through."

Steff didn't argue. For one thing she was too embarrassed by the lavish praise to say anything. For another she did think it was true that she saw the best in people and so helped bring that to the surface. She had with Tyler. She'd seen how good looking he was, and how charming he could be, and allowed him to dazzle her. She'd seen how confident he was, how assertive, and allowed herself to be swept along by him.

That evening she said, "Tyler, I want to talk to you about what I want. My job, where to live, a family."

"I know all that, babe."

"I don't think you …" She trailed off as he answered his phone.

As he discussed his team's chances of winning the next match, Steff's thoughts drifted back to her conversation with Ashley.

Her friend was wrong. Tyler wasn't a bully, but he didn't put her first. He wanted them to live somewhere which suited him and hadn't even considered them staying in the tiny house she loved. He'd just assumed, as many people did, that she'd want to have children and therefore need somewhere bigger. He'd not asked if that was the case. He hadn't even bothered explaining the rules of football so she could try to enjoy the sport he loved.

Ashley had also been right. Steff should leave Tyler, and she'd tell him her decision just as soon as he paid her enough attention to listen.

Like conkers, life was a game which could be played with many variations. She couldn't win it following someone else's preferences, by having her own ignored. She could only succeed by being the real Steff.

22. Fairy Pools

"Granny!" Freya exclaimed. "I saw one! I saw a real live fairy!"

"Oh!"

"Did you see her, Granny?"

"No, love." It was true, I hadn't seen a real fairy. I'd not looked at the doll either, but had taken it out my pocket and briefly held it behind my granddaughter's head as she looked into the fairy pool.

Freya practically danced around the little pool, trying to catch another glimpse. Lack of success did nothing to dampen her enthusiasm. If anything, the fact that it had completely vanished seemed to confirm to her the fairy had been real. "Do you think she did magic?" Freya asked.

"What do you think, love?"

"Yes! Fairies do magic. Let's look to see if there are more." She held my hand and urged me to negotiate further up the steep path and peer into the pools made by the tumbling stream. With her, the climb didn't seem hard. She's so like I was at that age that she doesn't just remind me what it was like to be young, she makes me feel young again.

At one point we had to take quite a big step in my case, and small jump in hers, to cross the water. Freya did it with confidence. A bit further on we had to scramble over boulders. Perched on the largest, she laughed about needing my help to get down. Fearlessly she rounded bends in the path, seeking out the unknown until we were right at the top of the gentle waterfall and able to look down on the route we'd taken. There were good views of the woods to either side, and more hills behind us.

"We're so high!" she marvelled. "It's almost like flying."

We spread our arms wide, as though we were eagles, and twisted about, imaging swooping our way back down the path. Not having wings of either feathers or gossamer, we made do with walking back towards the car. At least I did.

On all but the steepest bits Freya skipped, eager to return to the spot where she'd seen her fairy. Such a difference from how she'd been not twenty-four hours previously. And from how I gather she'd been the last few weeks.

My daughter-in-law, Lily, rang last week to confirm the details of Freya's stay with me. She and my son Paul were off on an adventure holiday and I was to have darling Freya to myself for two whole weeks.

"The timing is perfect," Lily said. "Things haven't been right …"

"What's happened? Is everything OK with you and Paul?"

"We're fine, honestly. Really looking forward to the trek, but you're right, something has happened."

"To Freya?"

"Don't worry, she's not hurt, but a couple of weeks ago she saw an accident. Our young neighbour came off one of those electric scooter things right in front of the house. He'd been carrying a bottle, so there was red wine everywhere."

"Oh dear. Was he badly hurt?"

"Thankfully just a few bruises, but Drax was obviously in pain and it was a shock to Freya."

"Did you say Drax? Freya has mentioned him, but as she said he's a wizard I didn't realise he was real."

"He's real alright, and really is a wizard of sorts. He works as a stage magician. She's seen him doing magic tricks. Quite often he produces little gifts for her, apparently from thin air. She'd have been upset to see anyone hurt, but it being Drax really dented her confidence."

I could understand that. Freya's a big fan of magic. The kind which makes everything bright and happy and fun. Anywhere we saw hoof prints but no horses, she announced unicorns were about and knew we'd have a lovely day.

"It's a shame for her to lose her belief in magic when she's still so young," I said.

"It's worse than that. Her optimism has gone and little things sometimes worry her out of all proportion. Paul and I are hoping being with you and having a change of scene will help."

"Don't worry, Lily. I'm sure it will."

I didn't tell Lily something similar had happened to me when I was about Freya's age. My big brother fell out of a tree. He'd only been winded, but seeing him land with a thud and then not move really frightened me. John, five years older than me, had been my hero. He could do impossible things, such as ride a bicycle – with no hands! Make me laugh just by counting to three. Open a book and see stories in those tiny black shapes lined up across the page.

With John inert on the ground, it felt as though all the magic was gone from the world.

By the time Mum came running in response to my yells he was on his feet and to look at him you'd think nothing had happened. But I knew. If a bad thing could happen to John, they could happen to anyone. I became scared to try anything new, to be left alone even in my bedroom and I stopped believing in magic. John tried to reassure me, but when he told me the funny things horses were thinking I knew he was making it up.

I don't remember how long I was upset and fearful. Probably not long, but a few days last forever if you're an unhappy seven-year-old. My granny took me to stay with her, in the cottage where I now live. We visited the fairy pools and I actually saw a fairy. Now I know that couldn't have happened, but she seemed so real. She was dressed in red and gold and had long flowing hair. Her gossamer wings fluttered so fast I hardly saw them. She had a musical, tinkling laugh and her smile made it impossible to be unhappy.

Years later I found a similar doll in Granny's cottage. She must have held it up behind me as I looked in the fairy pool and I'd seen the reflection. The ripples made her seem to be dancing in the air and the tinkling laugh was the gushing water. Learning the truth didn't matter. I was by then a happy and confident young adult. Lots of things had contributed to that, including my granny's love and the sighting of my 'real' fairy.

Before Freya came to stay I bought a fairy doll. It wasn't the same as the red and gold one which now sits on the chest of drawers in my bedroom. It was much more convincing with dragonfly wings and short, dark, pixie hair. Maybe I should have taken it with me for luck on the journey down to collect her.

I'd allowed time for the roadworks, but when I got through those I was so pleased to be able to speed up a bit, I went past the turning for the service area where we were to meet. It wasn't far to a junction and I was only a little late, but I worried the delay might cause my family anxiety.

"Granny!" Freya yelled as she'd hurtled towards me. She threw herself into my arms and clung on tight. "I thought you were never going to come!"

I apologised for keeping her and her parents waiting.

"It's fine," Paul said. "We've not been here long ourselves and you had to get through roadworks."

Freya's parents reassured her they would call often in a way which suggested they'd already made that promise several times. When I suggested things we might do during her visit she asked three times if I'd be with her the whole time. She also asked if she could sleep in the bedroom next to mine. The last time she'd stayed, with her parents, she'd been delighted to have the attic space to herself, declaring it to be like a princesses's tower.

"Of course you can, love," I said. "And I'll leave my door open, so you can come into my room anytime you like."

We went for a nice walk together, stopping for a fish supper which we ate from the paper, before returning by a longer route. As I'd intended, the walk wore Freya out. I put her to bed soon after we got back. She wanted stories and goodnight kisses, but she always does. She also wanted the light left on, which wasn't something she'd requested before.

"Of course. It will be nice for your dolls and teddies to see to play."

She liked that idea and was further cheered by a call from her parents wishing her goodnight.

Of course I didn't mind about the light, other than being slightly worried by Freya wanting it, but with my door open it created strange shadows.

As I walked into my room something fairy shaped seemed to fly across my bed. Despite retracing my steps I couldn't quite work out how my doll, sitting on the chest of drawers, could have cast such a clear shadow. The window was closed and the only sound was Freya's tinkling laugh, so I knew no unfortunate bird or bat was trapped in the house.

I slept well and it seemed Freya did too. She was almost back to her normal happy self when I suggested a trip to the fairy pools. Then she spilled milk on her dress and got in a state over it.

"Don't worry, love. You've got lots of other things to wear and I'll give this a rinse now so it will be dry when we get back." I wrapped her in what I declared was a magic cloak to keep her clean while she finished breakfast.

"It's just a towel, Granny."

She was quiet on the drive to the fairy pools and waited for me to tell her it was OK to get out of the car. That was good really, as she has a tendency to leap eagerly out of the child seat the moment the vehicle stops and can be a danger to other car park users or their paintwork. It was good too that she didn't rush up to hug the big dog we saw on the footpath, but I didn't like the way she got behind me and squeezed my hand tightly.

At the start of the climb up to the fairy pools there are stepping stones to be negotiated. They protrude several inches from the water level and are quite far apart if you have little legs, so I'd expected Freya would want to hold my hand. That didn't happen. I had to step down into the shallow water and carry her across. Even getting her to agree to that took some coaxing.

Once over she was relatively keen to make the climb up to the first of the series of pools, and even said how pretty it looked. I coaxed her to look into the turquoise water, and fumbled for the fairy doll I had with me. Just as I raised it over her shoulder, I heard people coming up behind us and put it away from fear they'd say something and unwittingly reveal what I was doing. Even so she gave a start.

"Granny, did you see something?"

I told her how the different minerals in the stones make the water pretty colours, and the different drops between the pools make the water swirl about creating patterns as it sparkles in the sun. When we were alone again, I took the doll from my pocket a second time.

I hesitated. Although I wanted to help Freya, was it right to try to trick her? I debated with myself that it was no different from talking about Santa and began to lift my arm. Then I considered her possible reaction to discovering I was pretending magic was real. I slipped the doll back into my pocket.

"Granny!" Freya exclaimed. "I saw one! I saw a real live fairy!"

I acted surprised, which was easy as I hadn't thought I'd lifted it high enough for her to see.

Freya told me she thought the fairy had done magic, and seeing the immediate difference in my granddaughter I was sure she was right. She had me exploring every inch of the steep and twisting paths, right up to where we spread our arms like eagle's wings.

When we got back down again she held my hand as we crossed the first few stepping stones together, then did the last couple, and the bigger jump up onto the bank, all by herself.

"Gosh, child," a man said. "You looked like you were flying!"

"That's because I have a fairy to help me," Freya said.

He laughed and so did I as I knew for sure that my darling Freya was back to her happy, magical self. Our mood only improved when we got back home and I received a text message.

Hi. I'm Drax. Heard how upset Freya was to see my tumble. Like to show her I'm OK.

I called him back and Freya and I watched him pull what seemed like thousands of silk scarves from a small envelope. He threw each over his shoulder where they fluttered in the breeze.

"Like fairies!" Freya said. "But real ones are even more beautiful."

"Oh, and how many real ones have you seen?" Drax asked.

"I think it was just one. She was in my room last night and then I saw her today in the fairy pool. I want to go and see her again tomorrow."

"You won't need to," Drax said. "If you've seen a fairy, then she's your special fairy and will be with you always."

He sounded as though he knew that for a fact, so when Freya asked if that was true, I didn't like to contradict him. "You said he's a wizard, love. Wizards would know about things like that."

I didn't give Freya the doll until I'd taken her back to where her parents were meeting us.

"Thank you, she's really pretty."

"Have you seen her before?" I asked.

Freya shook her head as she danced her along the car seat.

"Not at the fairy pools?"

"No. That was a real fairy!"

"What did she look like?"

"So beautiful! She wore a red and gold dress and had long hair and tiny little wings which flapped really fast."

"Oh!"

Before I could say more her parents arrived and there were hugs and gifts, and constant chatter over lunch. Everyone told everyone else what a lovely time they'd had. I could see how pleased and relieved Paul and Lily were at the change in their daughter. I didn't explain as I was sure Freya would tell them all about her fairy on the drive home.

When I got back to the cottage I went in search of my own fairy doll. I pulled open my bedroom door and looked straight across at the chest of drawers. She wasn't there!

That explained what Freya had seen. I must somehow have put her and not the one I'd bought for Freya, into my coat pocket. I'd been so worried about her, and thinking back to events from my past, so the mistake was understandable. As I'd not looked when I'd lifted her above Freya's shoulder at the fairy pools, I hadn't noticed. She must still be in my pocket.

She was. I felt rather guilty for having left her there all that time. The poor thing was worn and fragile and her once bright clothing faded. She was still beautiful I thought as I put her back in her rightful place. At the doorway I turned to look at her. The door to the next bedroom was still open, but the light wasn't on so I can't explain why I still saw a fairy shaped shadow flit across the room. Whatever the trick of light was, it worked its magic on my doll too and just for a moment she looked new and bright and absolutely real.

23. Gilbert Won't Make You Sick

Dominic and his little brother Gilbert were beginning to get on each other's nerves. They normally got on well together at home, mostly because they kept out of each other's way. That wasn't possible in the tiny caravan. Bad weather, during the family holiday in Devon, meant they were stuck inside for hours on end. Gilbert's games were too childish for Dominic, and anything which interested Dominic was too complicated for Gilbert.

Dominic was wishing he'd never agreed to come. He hadn't planned to, but his mum talked him round at the last minute.

"We hardly get to see you, now that you're at college. We all miss you, especially Gilbert. You know how he's always looked up to you."

"OK, OK, I'll come."

Dominic had imagined a week in the sun, showing his eight-year-old brother how to skim stones and study marine life trapped in rock pools. He'd thought fondly of racing Gilbert up and down the beach, making sure he only just beat him. He thought they'd mess around with the dinghy and build enormous sandcastles. That would all have been fun, they'd both have enjoyed that. Dominic wouldn't even have minded taking care of his brother, so his parents could spend some time together doing whatever they wanted to do. It hadn't worked out like that. Relentless heavy rain meant they'd all been stuck inside playing endless games of snakes and ladders, and beat they neighbour.

They boys' parents asked Dominic to mind Gilbert while they went shopping. "We'll get some magazines for you both and ask around to see if there's anywhere indoors we can visit."

"Good idea, Mum," Dominic said. He didn't think being shut in with Gilbert on his own would be any worse than it would be with the four of them. He was wrong. First the younger boy asked countless questions about stupid stuff, then he started whining that he was bored. The brothers were soon bickering.

"Dom, you're really boring now you're grown up. Why can't we do something interesting?"

"Just shut up, you make me sick!" Dominic shouted at Gilbert.

Gilbert's eyes filled with tears. "I'm sorry, Dom. I just thought we'd have adventures and stuff."

Fortunately their parents came back at that point. The magazines and comics cheered the boys up and the argument was soon forgotten.

The following day the weather was considerably better. The boys made up for lost time and ran around exploring the beach, building a sand fort, and trying to catch seagulls. When they eventually sat down to rest, Gilbert had pieces of seaweed stuck to his skin.

"You look like a sea monster!" Dominic said. He laughed as he brushed some of it off his brother.

"Yeah, well you look like a banana!"

"What are you on about now?"

"You look all yellow, Dom. Even your eyeballs."

"Yeah, right – and your tongue is bright blue!"

"Really?" Gilbert tried to stick his tongue out far enough to see it.

Energy restored, the boys climbed over rocks looking for hidden treasure until they got hungry, then raced back to the caravan. Gilbert almost won.

"What on earth has happened to you two?" their mum demanded.

"It's just seaweed, Mum. Dominic said my tongue's bright blue, but it isn't really, is it?"

"No it's not, little brother. I just said that because you said I'd turned yellow."

"You have!"

Mum told Dominic to look in the bathroom mirror. He wasn't quite the colour of a banana, but he really was yellow.

"It looks like jaundice," Mum said. "Do you feel alright?"

"Yes. I thought Gilbert was joking!"

Dad had been looking something up on his phone. "I think you're right about Dom having jaundice. There's a drop-in centre at the hospital – I think we should take him there to be checked over."

"In an ambulance?" Gilbert asked, clearly excited at the idea.

"No, son. We'll take the car."

Waiting to see a doctor was pretty boring, so Dominic didn't really blame his family for all coming into the examination room with him. It was good really as it meant he only had to answer the doctor's questions, not explain everything to them afterwards. The doctor asked even more questions than Gilbert tended to! She wanted to know how he felt, what he'd eaten and been doing lately. She looked at his skin and in his eyes and felt his stomach. It was rumbling really loudly.

"That's just because I've not had any tea," Dominic said. "We were going to, but came here instead. I'm starving!"

"And me!" Gilbert said.

"Hush, Gilbert love," Mum told him.

"You name is Gilbert? That's a coincidence as I think your big brother has Gilbert's disease." The doctor looked at Dominic. "We'll need to do a blood test to be sure, as there are other types of jaundice. I'll take a sample now."

"You mean I made him sick?" Gilbert asked.

"No, no. Gilbert is the name of the person who discovered this condition. Really I should have said Gilbert's syndrome as it's not actually a disease at all."

"I'm not worried about the name," Dominic said. "I just want to know if you can cure me."

"No, I can't – but don't worry as there's no need."

"What do you mean, no need?" Mum asked.

"Gilbert's syndrome rarely has any symptoms. This mild jaundice is most likely as bad as it's going to get. Although it might recur, it's only temporary and it won't damage your health, Dominic." As she spoke, the doctor wiped Dominic's arm and took a small sample of blood.

"How did he get it?" Dad asked. "Will we all go down with it?"

"It's not contagious. It's actually hereditary, so I expect one of you already has it. You easily could without being aware of the fact. Gilbert's syndrome is quite common, it's estimated that around one in twenty people have it."

"If it's not a disease, what exactly is it?" Dominic asked.

"It's a build up of a chemical called bilirubin. Everyone produces it in their haemoglobin."

"Is that the stuff which carries oxygen in our blood?' Dominic asked.

"That's right, yes. In people with Gilbert's syndrome the bilirubin isn't broken down as as quickly as it is in people who don't have the condition. Usually that doesn't matter, but just occasionally it causes jaundice. That most often happens if the person has been ill or stressed, or as in your case if you've been physically active."

Dominic had been a bit stressed, but he didn't say so. Gilbert had been unusually quiet since hearing what this syndrome was called. Dominic didn't want him worrying he was to blame for causing it, not after losing his temper and saying his little brother made him sick. "Will Gilbert get it too?"

"That's quite possible. Boys are more likely to get it than girls, but really it's nothing to worry about."

"Not unless his tongue goes blue, right?"

"Blue? Let me see."

Gilbert obligingly stuck his tongue right out.

"That looks fine, but just to be on the safe side, eat lots of vegetables and clean your teeth every night before bed," the doctor said.

"What happens now?" Mum asked.

"I'll send of the blood sample for testing. If, as I strongly suspect, there are raised levels of bilirubin with no signs of liver liver problems, that will indicate Gilbert's syndrome.

I'll make sure your own GP is informed of the results. You can call the surgery in about ten days for the outcome."

"Thank you, but what I really meant is what difference it will make to Dominic's life?"

"As he's well in himself there's no need to make any changes to your holiday plans, unless he shows any other symptoms. If that should happen you can either bring him back here or contact your GP if you're home. If it is Gilbert's disease then Dominic won't need to make any changes. If the test shows it's not Gilbert's syndrome then more tests will be needed and your GP will advise on the next steps. In the meantime, please enjoy the rest of your holiday."

"Does Dominic have to eat vegetables too?" Gilbert asked.

"Absolutely!"

As the family drove away from the hospital, they discussed what to have for their supper.

"Aw, Mum, I was hungry hours ago." Dominic said. "I don't think I can listen to you talking about food, then smell you cooking it, without chewing Gilbert's arm off!"

"Don't let him eat me, Mum," Gilbert said, pretending to be afraid.

"How about me stop for fish and chips?" Dad suggested. "Oh, and better get some mushy pease with it!"

As soon as Dad stopped the car, the boys raced to the chip shop. Gilbert very nearly won.

24. Bald Truth

The man sitting opposite Jenny had a shiny, bald head. It didn't matter. Jenny hadn't expected everyone at the speed dating event to be utterly gorgeous and perfect in every way. She wasn't herself, despite what her sister said.

Although Jenny didn't want to be there and had zero interest in a proper date, she didn't want the man thinking she'd ruled him out at first glance. He might well be a nice person, but if she dented his confidence maybe that wouldn't shine through. She mustered what courage she had, plastered on a smile and said, "Hi, I'm Jenny."

"Bill," he replied, shaking her hand.

"You seem familiar. Have we …"

"You're thinking of this guy." He produced a newspaper clipping of Prince William.

"Oh, of course. Sorry."

"It's OK, happens a lot. That's why I shorten my name and, when my hair started receding, I shaved it all off. I can cope with people being put off by my lack of hair, but not the disappointment there's no crown to disguise it."

"I'm not disappointed. Dating a member of the royal family wouldn't suit me at all. I hate being in the limelight."

"Which is why you're sitting with your back to the room?"

"Yeah. I don't like people looking at me."

"So, what do you like?"

By the time they discovered he didn't share her fondness for cheesy one hit wonders, the bell went and he moved on. Jenny put a tick by No1 on her card. As she'd told Louise, she really didn't want a date but she'd promised to be open minded and would get a scolding for nothing but crosses. Besides, she was fairly certain he wasn't interested in her.

The next man to sit opposite Jenny was also completely bald. Odd coincidence.

He introduced himself as Mark. "What's a nice girl like you doing in a place like this?" he asked, with a grin.

"Would you believe me if I said I was hoping for a date?"

"Not really. I saw you arrive."

"Oh." That meant he'd seen Louise practically force her into the pub. "She's my sister and thought this would be a good idea."

"I'm here for the same reason," Mark said.

"We're more the same than you realise," Jenny said.

"Oh?"

"Sorry, just thinking aloud."

"And trying not to stare at my head."

Jenny admitted it. "Coincidence, after the last guy."

"A lot of people are bald, for lots of different reasons."

"I suppose …"

"As I told my niece, when her hair started coming out during chemo, it's not something to be ashamed of and doesn't mean you won't be loved."

"Poor kid."

"She's been through a lot, but seems past the worst. I promised to stay bald as long as she is and …" Mark showed her his phone. The little girl had a soft fuzz of pale blonde on her head.

"She's recovering? That's wonderful!"

"It is. What's your favourite food?" he asked.

"Food?" Jenny was momentarily thrown by the change of subject.

Mark waved his speed dating match card. "In case I get lucky. Wouldn't want to put you off by suggesting we go for pizza if you can't stand it."

"I love it… with pineapple."

"Pineapple? On pizza?" He made a big show of putting a tick against her name on his match card.

Laughing, Jenny did the same on hers. She could just picture the expression on her foodie sister's face when told that's what the date would involve.

They chatted about terrible tastes for a while. Mark confessed a fondness for corduroy.

"That's nothing. Half my clothes are covered in diamanté or sequins." The half she no longer wore, because she didn't like being noticed these days.

"Then I hope to be dazzled on our date."

The next guy was also totally bald. Jenny swung round and realised none of the men present had hair. She strode to the middle of the room, "What's going on?"

Mark rushed over. "Please, none of us wanted to upset you. We thought this would help. Your sister …"

"Louise put you up to this?" He had said he was there for the same reason as her, but she'd thought he meant someone had talked him into it.

"She's been searching for bald men and set up this evening. She thought if you saw beyond our bald heads to the people underneath, you'd realise you don't need to hide your own baldness in order for people to like you."

What nice people. Judging from their conversations so far they'd given up more than a couple of hours in front of the TV to help make Jenny feel better about her alopecia. They went out, had friends, enjoyed life. Maybe Louise was right and Jenny wouldn't be shunned by the entire world simply because of her condition.

Jenny pulled off her wig. Instead of gasps of shock, she heard a round of applause.

"Thanks, everyone. I'll put this back on now, but I'm not going to keep shutting myself away."

"Good for you, love," said a man Jenny hadn't yet talked to. "Now, can we get on with the dates? I'm never going to get a better chance."

"But… This isn't real?" Jenny asked.

"Actually it is," a young woman called out. "Louise arranged the whole thing. Some of us woman have hair loss too and we all knew we'd be meeting men who are temporarily or permanently bald."

"Oh." Jenny resumed her seat where her remaining dates explained they were – a wig model who found it easier to have no hair of his own, an actor who'd shaved his head for a role, two people with alopecia, one undergoing chemotherapy, a guy who'd suffered an accident at work involving some kind of irritant and someone who'd removed his hair as an ecological protest.

Some Jenny quite liked, others not so much. That was fine – she couldn't expect to like every man she met on a speed dating event. It was good to realise her opinions weren't due to their lack of hair. It was even better to remember that Mark, who'd shaved his own head in order to prove to a little girl that baldness was nothing to be ashamed of and didn't mean you couldn't be loved, had put a tick by her name.

Thank you for reading this book. I hope you enjoyed it. If you did, I'd really appreciate a short review on Amazon, Goodreads – or anywhere else.

I can be found at www.patsycollins.co.uk You may like to sign up for my newsletter and get free stories, plus news of the latest releases, special offers, competitions and behind the scenes insights. A link can be found on the website, or you can use subscribepage.io/ItLSNa

More Books by Patsy Collins

Novels –

Little Mallow cosy mystery series –

Disguised Murder and Community Spirit in Little Mallow
Dependable Friends and Deceitful Neighbours in Little Mallow
Deadly Words and Innocent Gossip in Little Mallow

Other novels –

Firestarter
Escape To The Country
A Year And A Day
Paint Me A Picture
Leave Nothing But Footprints
Acting Like A Killer

Short story collection sets –

All That Love Stuff
With Love And Kisses
Lots Of Love
Love Is The Answer

Your Good Health

Over The Garden Fence
Up The Garden Path
Through The Garden Gate
In The Garden Air
Beyond The Garden Wall

No Family Secrets
Can't Choose Your Family
Keep It In The Family
Family Feeling
Happy Families

Slightly Spooky Stories I
Slightly Spooky Stories II
Slightly Spooky Stories III
Slightly Spooky Stories IV
Slightly Spooky Stories V

Criminal Intent
Crime In Mind

Other short story collections –

A Clean Bill Of Health

Just A Job

Patsy Collins

Perfect Timing

A Way With Words

Dressed To Impress

Coffee & Cake

Making A Move

Days To Remember

Not A Drop To Drink

Unearthing The Truth

Non-fiction –

From Story Idea To Reader
(co-written with Rosemary J. Kind)

A Year Of Ideas:
365 sets of writing prompts and exercises